A Lady's Guide to a Gentleman's Heart
Heart of a Scandal Series

Copyright © 2018 by Christi Caldwell

For more information about the author:
www.christicaldwellauthor.com
christicaldwellauthor@gmail.com
Twitter: @ChristiCaldwell
Or on Facebook at: Christi Caldwell Author

For first glimpse at covers, excerpts, and free bonus material, be sure to sign up for my monthly newsletter!

Printed in the USA.

Cover Design and Interior Format

© THE KILLION GROUP INC.

A Lady's Guide To A Gentleman's Heart

Heart of a
Scandal
SERIES

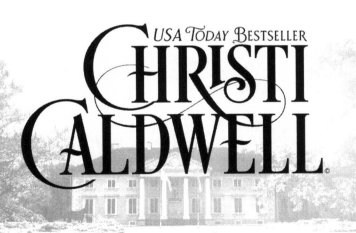

USA Today Bestseller

Christi Caldwell

Other Titles by
Christi Caldwell

HEART OF A DUKE
In Need of a Duke—Prequel Novella
For Love of the Duke
More than a Duke
The Love of a Rogue
Loved by a Duke
To Love a Lord

THE HEART OF A SCOUNDREL
To Wed His Christmas Lady
To Trust a Rogue
The Lure of a Rake
To Woo a Widow
To Redeem a Rake
One Winter with a Baron
To Enchant a Wicked Duke
Beguiled by a Baron
To Tempt a Scoundrel

THE HEART OF A SCANDAL
In Need of a Knight—Prequel Novella
Schooling the Duke

LORDS OF HONOR
Seduced by a Lady's Heart
Captivated by a Lady's Charm
Rescued by a Lady's Love
Tempted by a Lady's Smile

A REGENCY DUET
Rogues Rush In

MEMOIR: NON-FICTION
Uninterrupted Joy

PROLOGUE

Kent, England
Winter, 1821

ONE MIGHT SAY HEATH WHITWORTH, the Marquess of Mulgrave, knew better than anyone when his mother, the Duchess of Sutton, was up to something.

For there could be no doubting…she was up to something.

And it was all because of that note she'd held in her fingers since he'd entered his father's office. Folding the page she'd just read to him along its pointed crease, she neatly rested it on her husband's immaculate desk. "Married. Our son is married."

"Your youngest son," Heath felt inclined to point out. He had decidedly married no one, and for that matter, had no intentions of doing so any time soon.

His droll announcement was swiftly ignored by his parents.

"Say it's the Aberdeen girl," his father gritted out.

The Aberdeen girl. Heath's back went up, as it always did with any mention or sight of his mother's goddaughter. Even a mention of Lady Emilia Aberdeen could never be good.

"Oh, come, Samuel. That does not make sense. Lady Emilia arrived earlier this afternoon with her parents and occupied the second chair from yours not even five hours ago. It could hardly be Emilia."

And through it, the lady had looked as hopelessly bored as Heath himself. Who'd have imagined the two of them would have *anything* in common.

"Are you making light of... of... this?" his father was saying.

Now, this was much safer talk—mention of his brother Sheldon's hasty marriage to a young widow with three children. Nonetheless, Heath cast a quick glance over his shoulder, considering the best path to escape. After all, there'd been talk of Emilia Aberdeen and that never proved good...in any way.

"Hardly, Samuel. I'd never dare jest about Emilia's unwed state or our son's recently wedded one."

A vein bulged at the corner of his father's right eye. The duke's cheeks had gone red with angry color. His father fought for control of his temper.

This was the time for Heath to make his escape.

Heath shoved back his chair. "I'm not entirely certain my being here—"

"Sit," his mother ordered, ending his hope of flight.

Bloody hell. Heath resettled himself back into his seat.

"Now," she went on in her attempt at more measured tones, as she smoothed her skirts, "this requires attention from *each* of us. Whether you approve or not, Samuel, your son has married by special license." The duke growled. "And the world is already abuzz with that news."

"How can the world be abuzz?" Samuel waved the fast-wrinkling scrap about. "By the accounts of this, he's been married just three days."

Once more his parents launched into a debate about their just-married, younger son. Waiting...waiting, and then finding his window, he pounced. "Perhaps I should allow you both—"

His parents spoke in unison. "Sit."

Yanking at his cravat, Heath fell back in his seat. "Damned younger brothers." And damned responsibilities that went with being a ducal heir. One's life was not one's own. No part of it. His presence in the midst of one of his parents' rows was proof enough of that.

His mother turned a frown on him. "I beg your pardon?"

This time, he was wise enough to fall silent, and thankfully she redirected her ire and energies back to her husband.

Through it, Heath's guard remained up. He'd been summoned

here…for a reason. And no summons from his mother could ever be a good one.

Not when Emilia Aberdeen's name was mentioned.

"Now, for the second reason behind this family meeting…" His muscles tensed. It was coming… "There is the awkwardly uncomfortable matter of Lady Emilia Aberdeen."

Heath snapped his brows together. And there it was. Emilia Aberdeen. She proved the reason Heath was here. It was inevitable. After all, Heath's mother, best friend to Emilia's mother, had been trying to marry the chit off since she'd been thrown over… by Heath's best friend.

"What about her?" his father was asking impatiently.

"Well, all the guests have already suspected and whispered about our trying to coordinate a match between Emilia and Sheldon."

Because that is precisely what his mother had been doing: trying to marry off her younger, more affable, son to her beloved goddaughter. Only to have been thwarted by Sheldon's marrying another.

"We've inadvertently made Emilia the gossip of the house party."

"Which will all be forgotten when Sheldon and his bride arrive," he quickly put in, grasping at any out available to him.

His mother turned a stare on him.

He resisted the urge to squirm. Too obvious. He'd been too forceful with his previous assurance.

"Nonetheless, it stands to reason that none should suspect that she was here intending to be matched with Sheldon. After all, she's already suffered a scandal no lady ought." Betrothed to the Duke of Renaud; and Heath's only friend in the world. The other man had broken it off with Lady Emilia years ago.

Emilia had paid the price in gossip ever since.

His stomach muscles clenched. *I will not feel badly. I will not feel badly*… That was after all, what his mother wished.

"I'd simply ask that you give Emilia some attention," his mother said evenly, and he started, having failed to realize he'd been thinking aloud.

"Attention," he echoed dumbly. Oh, this was bad. Nay, worse than he'd feared.

"Some indication that mayhap it was you we'd intended for her to make a match with, and then…"

Heath choked, the strangled cough cutting off his reply. His mother crossed over and thumped him between the shoulder blades.

"You want me to court her?" he managed between wheezes.

"I want you to simply act as though she is... someone you want to be around." *Never.* "It's the least you can do."

That brought him up short. What in blazes was that supposed to mean? "What in blazes did *I* do?" he shouted.

"Your best friend is, after all, the one who jilted her."

Damned Renaud. On the heel of that came a flood of guilt for the friend who'd had to break it off for reasons the world didn't know. Not even Lady Emilia. Be that as it may... "*I* didn't jilt the lady." Heath spoke through gritted teeth. "I hardly know the lady." *Liar.* You know she's spirited and witty and—

"All this I-I-I, Heath. Really. Furthermore," she continued, "it speaks a good deal to your snobbishness. We've been family friends with the Duke of Gayle since before your birth. You've known Emilia since she was in Leading strings. The least you can do is be friendly to the girl."

Emilia wasn't a girl. Not any longer. She was a woman more vibrant than the sunny creature she'd been as a child. "The girl is nearly thirty."

"All I'm asking is that you be friendly with her. If she's alone... see that she has company. Take the gossip off of Sheldon's desertion and make Society question whether you, in fact, are the one with intentions towards her."

His cravat was choking at him. Nay, his mother's request was. He made a desperate appeal to the only one to make her see reason. "Mad, Father. Tell her she's gone utterly insane."

His father would choose that moment to go silent.

So there would be no help coming from *that* quarter. Or it would appear any...

"You both have your instructions," Heath's mother said, snapping her skirts. "Kindness... towards your son and his new family," she directed at her husband. "And *you* towards Lady Emilia," she said to Heath.

As she exited, Heath fell back in his chair.

His mother could hand out all the directives she wished. The last thing he wished to do was spend the holiday or any day, for that matter, entertaining Lady Emilia Aberdeen—his mother's wishes be damned.

CHAPTER 1

*No relationship can be built on a betrayal. That is,
no relationship that is worth having.*
Mrs. Matcher
A Lady's Guide to a Gentleman's Heart

Winter 1821
Kent
Later that week...

LORD HEATH WHITWORTH, THE MARQUESS of Mulgrave, had been trapped.

Not even for the first, nor second, nor third time. And in each instance, he found himself trapped by the usual suspect: his mother, the Duchess of Sutton.

This time, however, she was here for business.

Nor was his observation a figurative thought surmised from the determined glint in her eyes. She was literally before him bearing an official-looking paper.

That look combined with that page could only portend doom.

As such, there was just one thing a gentleman could do under such circumstances—go on the offense.

Folding his arms at his chest, he stared across the opposite end of the billiards table at her. "No."

His mother crossed her own arms in a matching pose. The paper in her fingers dangled at her forearm. "I've not said anything."

Yet. "Nor did you need to," he put in smoothly. "Whatever you're asking, I trust the safest answer is 'no.'"

"For shame, Heath." She gave him a hurt look. "Can't I simply pay a visit to my son?"

"In the *billiards room*? In the middle of your house party with a sea of guests off in one of your many parlors, no less?" Given all that, he'd have to be a damned fool to believe—even with that wounded expression she'd donned—that there was anything less than mercenary in her presence here.

Just like that, the façade ended. His mother sharpened her gaze. "Very well. You'd prefer me to be direct."

He hitched his hip onto the corner of the billiards table and with his spare hand urged her to have out with it. After all, he'd long ceased to be surprised, shocked, or horrified by his mother's directives. "I'm listening."

"I would like you to show Lady Emilia a good time."

He lost his balance and landed hard on his arse.

Frowning, his mother came to stand over him. "I thought I'd been clear," she went on, relentless. "And please stand this instant, Heath. I feel rather silly having this discussion with you sprawled on the floor."

Really, this was what she found silly? And not the whole ordering him to show a respectable lady *a good time*?

"Well?" his mother demanded after he'd taken to his feet.

"You," he began slowly, "want me to…" No. No matter how many times he attempted, he couldn't force out the words ordered by his mother about this particular woman—ever. He found the nearest chair.

"You are usually far more clever than this, dear boy," his mother chided, her disapproving tone making abundantly clear the endearment was really an insult. "I asked you to show her a good time."

And there it was again. He cringed, for the fourth time since she'd stolen his blessed solitude.

And by the way she'd planted herself in front of him—arms folded—she was prepared for battle.

Heath tamped down a groan and peered around her at the door, contemplating escape.

His mother slid sideways, ending all hope of that endeavor. She clapped her hands once. "Do attend me. I asked you at the beginning of the house party to—"

Blast and damn. He sat upright in his seat. "Show her a good time. Yes, yes. I've quite heard you." But hearing that order from his mother numerous times was enough to turn a man's stomach worse than rancid kippers washed down with a glass of vinegar. "If you are interested in someone seeing to that particular goal, you'd be wise to consult Sheldon." His younger brother by two years had long ago earned a reputation as a rogue.

His mother flicked his ear, and he cursed. "Bloody hell, that—*oww*," he grunted as she gave it another flick. "What in blazes was that for?"

"The first was because you know your brother is newly and happily married and quite reformed."

"And the other?" he groused, rubbing at the wounded lobe.

"Because of the cursing. Now, you very well know Sheldon cannot be the one to"—he tensed—"make Emilia's time here enjoyable." He relaxed at that less vulgar substitute.

"She, I suspect, would be entirely more appreciative if I am not the one to make her time enjoyable."

"Emilia."

"I assure you I know who we're talking about." His mother had been quite clear in her requests of Heath since the damned winter party had commenced. "How could I not know who we're speaking of?" he drawled.

His mother snorted. "Are you certain, Heath? Are you truly certain, because since I found your hiding spot fifteen minutes ago, you've not managed to mention her name even once?"

"I'd hardly call the billiards room a hiding spot. Now, if I sought to hide, I'd seek out the former cellars or—the conservatory." While he spoke, he angled his head ever so slightly, waiting for his moment.

"I know what you are doing, young man. And I assure you… it is not going to work."

At thirty-two years of age, Heath hadn't been a "young man" in more than a decade. "Tell me, Mother," he drawled, "just what is it that I'm trying to do?"

She shifted, and Heath came quickly to his feet. He gave the door another longing look before making a beeline for the drink cart. His mother might be two decades his senior and wearing a gown and silk slippers, but she'd proven she could outrace any of her children at any age when she wished it.

"Avoid her," she said flatly. "You are trying to avoid her."

Yes, well, she had him there.

"I made myself clear when I asked you—"

"Ordered me."

"—to pay Emilia some attention," she continued over his interruption.

Heath poured himself a tall snifter of brandy, focusing all his attentions on the simple task. "I am most likely the last person she—"

"Emilia."

"—would care to spend her days, let alone a single moment, with." He set the bottle down and faced his mother once more. "In fact, in case it has escaped your notice, the lady hasn't exchanged a word with me"—in years—"since she arrived."

His mother furrowed her brow. "Are we speaking of the same woman? Because you've still not brought yourself to utter her name *once* since she arrived."

This again. "Ohhhh, I know her." At the duchess' pointed look, he sighed. *Touché.* "Very well, I know *Lady Emilia Aberdeen*," he amended. "Your goddaughter." The girl he'd always been tongue-tied around when they were children. "The Duke and Duchess of Gayle's daughter. And my best friend's"—his mother was already across the room, a palm stretched out—"former betroff—" The duchess' hand muffled the remainder of his response, summarily knocking more than half the contents of his drink over the rim of his glass, soaking his fingers and his jacket.

Bloody hell.

"Hush this instant, Heath," she whispered, stealing a glance back at the door as if she feared the guests who'd already sought out the evening's entertainments might somehow be lurking outside the billiards room. She gave him a long, pointed look. "Am I free to remove this now?"

"Wuffsthealternative?" he mumbled into her gloved hand. "Suffocatin-meh." And by God, he'd bet his future title of duke that her fingers crept up a smidge to cover his nostrils.

"Now," she went on as she removed her hand, freeing him to

breathe once more. "You know we do not speak of him… at least around her." His mother flushed. "Emilia. Now, going forward, you'll refer to her by her name."

"Very well." Removing his kerchief, he snapped the immaculate fabric open and proceeded to mop up the excess moisture from his spilled drink. "As I was saying, given my friendship with her former betrothed, I hardly think I'm the person she'd care to keep company with"—*ever*—"for your house party." Nor was his supposition speculative in nature. At any Society event they'd attended together, she'd barely looked at him, let alone uttered a single word. In fairness, neither had he gone out of his way to have any face-to-face meetings with her. After all, Heath, by nature of who he'd always been, preferred life… to be uncomplicated, absent of discomfort. Emilia Aberdeen, with her broken betrothal and his continued friendship with the almost-groom, would rest alongside the dictionary definition of *discomfort*.

"Then *try*." His mother shoved something into his chest, and he grunted.

"What in blazes—"

She flicked his ear, earning another curse.

"It is a list," she said. "To help you."

To help him? Heath unfolded the scrap.

"Because you are not necessarily as charming as your brother."

"Why, thank you, Mother," he intoned dryly.

"Oh, hush. You've always said as much."

"I've said I am the serious one," he muttered, "which is altogether different."

"Is it, Heath?" She arched a brow in the manner that had terrified him as a boy. "Is it?"

No, it really wasn't. Regardless, wounded pride aside, there was some benefit to that low—if accurate—opinion of him.

"Very well," he conceded. "I'm not the charming one, which is also why I'm the absolute last person who should be assigned this task." And with that, he reached for his cue stick, marking an end to the nonsense she'd put to him.

His mother planted her hand on the velvet table, blocking his shot. "Emilia is certainly not a task."

"Do I want to keep company with her or…" He squinted down at the numbered list on the edge of the table. He promptly choked.

"Ask her what she'd like to spend her morn doing and then do it? The answer is decidedly no." Grabbing up the page, he handed it over to his mother. Or attempted to. She ignored his efforts, making no move to take the sheet.

"Read it."

With that curt order, he sighed and resumed reading. A strangled laugh escaped him, amusement shaking his frame. "You expect me to"—he glanced at item two—"woo a lady over breakfast? What in the Lord's name did you use to make this list?"

His mother bristled. "I'll have you know this is not amusing."

"Your Lady's Guide," he drawled.

"The Lady's Guide to a Gentleman's Heart is a most reliable source on how one should conduct oneself around a lady."

He snorted.

"Oh, hush," she chided, giving his arm a less-than-gentle tap that was more slap than anything. "Snobbishness hardly suits you."

He winced and rubbed the aggrieved flesh. The Duchess of Sutton, master of control, had turned bloodthirsty. This was even more dire than he'd feared. "Does snobbishness suit *any* person?" he drawled, and this time, he was quick enough to step away to avoid another assault on his person.

"I'll have you know this column you'd deride is all the rage."

"Either way, I've no desire to take part in any of this. Therefore, your words are, in fact, an order."

"You put that note in your pocket this instance, Heath."

Even as he knew he was being a childlike boor, Heath set it on the sideboard.

His mother breathed through her nose, slowly, evenly, and that was how he knew he'd crossed a line. "Very well, Heath. Leaving the list out is the wiser course, because the moment I step foot outside this room, you're going to memorize it, and thoroughly. Are we clear?" Not waiting for an answer, because the Duchess of Sutton would always know the definitive answer to that non-question question, she swept from the room and left him alone once more.

"We are clear," he muttered anyway after she'd gone.

Sometimes, he wished he'd been the recalcitrant of the Whitworth children; that he'd been the rogue of a brother who the Duke and Duchess had grown so accustomed to hearing 'no' from.

Because then mayhap he could have simply denied her orders and carried on with his own affairs. After his brother's death, the sense of obligation, the need to be everything his parents needed him to be, had become so ingrained in his character, Heath didn't know any other way.

If he had been less devoted to being a dutiful son, mayhap he'd have had the sense his younger brother had when he'd skipped out on the last house party that would have seen him playing partner to Lady Emilia.

Alas, duty always took precedence over all.

"Lady Emilia Aberdeen," he muttered into the quiet. And because Heath always was and would always be the dutiful son, he picked up that damned scrap and read the remainder of the tasks assigned to him.

2. She arises early for the morning meal. (Six o'clock punctually.) Break your fast with her.

Splendid, she was the one woman in the whole of England who didn't rise late. What was next?

3. Be a good conversationalist to her. Express an interest in whatever subject she speaks to you on. Ask questions. Ladies like to know people care about what they are talking about.

Be a good…? Heath glanced around the room, all but waiting for his mother to jump out and declare the list her grandest—albeit her only—jest. What in blazes was he supposed to speak with Emilia Aberdeen about? He, the least charming of the Whitworths, who'd rarely engaged in discourse with the lady, even when she'd been betrothed to his friend—and when she'd still possessed a sunny disposition. Shaking his head, he resumed reading.

4. Do try to make her laugh. She's still hurting.

"You're relying on the wrong son if you expect that," he mumbled.

5. If she seems upset, it is your gentlemanly responsibility and duty to somehow cheer her up.

That was rather redundant, and if his mother was about he'd take great pleasure and pointing as much out to her.

*6. Do **not**, under any circumstances, discuss her betrothal to that scoundrel you call friend.*

By the bold, starred, and heavily-underlined emphasis, item six was of the greatest significance on the whole damned list. And if his mother had still been here, he'd have delighted in pointing out that items four through six were more warnings than activities on her Emilia Aberdeen To-Do List.

Heath skimmed the list one more time. All requirements laid out for him. With, of course, several warnings of what *not* to do.

All he need do was entertain Lady Emilia and then the lady and her parents would head off to their own estates—and Heath would be spared.

Jamming the hated list inside his jacket, he exchanged the scrap for a long swallow of the brandy in the glass that had not spilled over the rim.

Then, gathering up his cue stick, he returned to his much-welcomed game of billiards—in blessed, solitary peace.

CHAPTER 2

*A lady's age does not define her or her worth, and any
gentleman who thinks it matters is no man whose affec-
tions you should seek…*
Mrs. Matcher
A Lady's Guide to a Gentleman's Heart

NEARLY TEN YEARS AGO, LADY Emilia Aberdeen had gone
from being almost a duchess, to a jilted bride.

The tale of her jilting had proven to be Society's favorite scandal
to drag forth whenever there were no new tastier on dits to con-
sume. After all, the world believed Emilia's heart was still crushed
beyond repair. It was why, even now, the guests in attendance at
the Duchess of Sutton's winter house party believed Emilia had
shut herself away in her rooms.

None, however, would dare suspect that Emilia was, in fact,
responsible for one of the most successful columns in the *London
Post*.

Tapping the corner of her lip, Emilia fished another letter from
a stack of five—

Alas, both peace and solitude proved altogether too short-lived.

"You had better be ill, Emilia Abernathy Aberdeen."

With a little shriek, Emilia jammed the handful of notes into
the back of her journal. The Duchess of Gayle stood framed in the
doorway. "Mother," she greeted.

"You do not appear ill to me, Emilia," her mother clipped out, closing the door with a measured calm that only a duchess could muster.

Emilia feigned a belated cough. "Mother," she repeated in faint tones.

Ever graceful, the Duchess of Gayle glided over, her silver satin skirts swirling about her ankles as she walked. "You are a horrid liar, which is a good thing." As if to punctuate that point, she tapped her fan atop the corner of Emilia's temporary desk.

Given the secrets she'd managed to keep from her mother, father, and younger brother, she'd rather venture she was a good deal more capable at subterfuge than any of the Aberdeens credited. Or mayhap they just wished to see something in her other than what was really there. "I simply sought some privacy."

"You've had ten years of privacy," her mother said with an unexpected bluntness about a topic no one spoke of, let alone danced around. "No one wants a melancholy wife, Emilia."

"Which is fine, as I've no wish to be anyone's wife."

Her mother snorted and rapped the desk again.

Emilia dragged her book protectively closer, folding her arms around the cherished pages.

"Do not be silly. Everyone wishes to be a wife. At least, eventually."

"Actually, I do not." At one point, she would have agreed with her mother. And at one point, Emilia had fit into that neat, societal mold. She'd desired a husband. Nay, not just any husband: a witty, charming, roguish man… And for a brief time, in her betrothed, she'd had him.

Until she hadn't. "I'm quite content with my circumstances." The blighter had broken it off by letter and marched himself off, traveling… wherever it was bounders traveled.

"I do not like what you've become, Emilia."

"And what is that?" she drawled. "More discerning?"

"More cynical," her mother said flatly.

Which was also, surprisingly, on the mark for her mother. Since that long-ago day, Emilia was more cynical. She was also wiser. More guarded. "I'm also more *content* with my current spinsterish circumstances."

Her mother choked and stole a glance at the doorway. "Hush.

You are not a… You are not a…" The duchess' lips moved, but this time no words came out.

"*Spiiinster.*" Emilia delighted in stretching out the two syllables.

"That one. You're not"—her mother gesticulated with a gloved fingertip, jabbing at the air—"*that.*"

"I'm nearing thirty years old, Mother."

Her mother slapped her hands over her ears. "Mm. Mmm. You're some years away from that."

Emilia lifted two fingers. "Two." When her obstinate parent refused to take her hands from her ears, Emilia waggled those digits under her nose.

"We are *not* talking about your age," she said, her voice slightly raised and discordant because her palms muted her hearing.

"Actually, we are," she said, cupping her hands around her mouth. "I was pointing out that I'm twenty-eight—"

"Do hush." The duchess at last let her arms fall to her sides. "We are talking about your marriage."

Which had been the purpose of the *last* house party she'd attended here at her godmother's. To coordinate a match between Emilia and the Duke and Duchess of Sutton's youngest son… a scapegrace son who'd hightailed it off to avoid that fate… and who'd instead found another young woman to marry.

Setting aside her book, Emilia stood. "I do not wish to marry. I am more than content with my life as it is."

Are you truly? Living with your parents still. All your friends scattered throughout England now, living their own lives.

While Emilia was escorted to the same events she'd been escorted to since she was a girl just out for her debut.

The duchess' eyes softened. "Oh, Emilia," she said with an uncharacteristic tenderness. "Eventually, you are going to find the man worthy of you. The one who makes you laugh and smile and love again."

"Thank you, Mama." Emilia studied the relaxed lines of her mother's ageless face. "But I still have no intention of joining the festivities this evening."

Her mother let out an unduchesslike squeal and yanked her hands back, the façade of earlier warmth shattered. "You are impossible, Emilia Abernathy. Impossible. Imp—" A knock at the door interrupted the third *impossible.*

There was another knock. This time, firmer and slightly impatient.

Smoothing her palms down the front of her skirts, the duchess swept over and, plastering a serene smile on her lips, drew it open. "Oh, you."

"Hardly the warmest of greetings for one's beloved son," Barry, Emilia's younger brother by two years, drawled.

"I'm in the midst of speaking to your sister about very important matters."

"Indeed?" Angling his head around the duchess, he mouthed, "Marriage?"

"What else?" she silently returned.

"Your sister"—as if there might be another sibling in question, the duchess slashed a hand in Emilia's direction—"is sitting in her rooms. Alone. Writing in that silly book. People are talking."

"Imagine preferring the company of oneself to a house full of Society's leading lords and ladies," Barry said dryly.

Emilia's lips twitched in amusement at the droll response.

"Precisely!"

A droll response that their mother did not properly discern.

Barry cleared his throat. "Never one to interfere in the ever-important discussion of Emilia's wedded state—"

"Unwedded, Barry. The state of your sister's circumstances is unwedded."

"I am, however, the dutiful godson," he went on over the interruption, "and promised Lady Sutton that I would see what kept you, as she was requesting your company."

Emilia's heart lifted. Saved by the least likely of rescuers—her younger brother. A rapscallion who'd previously taken great pleasure in tormenting her over the years.

"I love you," she mouthed.

He touched the corner of his eye. "You owe me," he whispered back.

The duchess continued on oblivious to that exchange. "Lady Caroline is looking for me? Why did you not say so immediately?" Because even as Emilia's spinster state took precedence over many issues, their mother's devotion to her obligations as a leading societal hostess and deference for rank trumped most. "Perhaps you'll speak to your sister and see if you can talk some sense into her."

Barry inclined his head and pressed a hand to his chest. "You have my word," he vowed with mock solemnity.

Emilia made a show of wiping some imagined speck from the corner of her mouth to hide another smile.

"I saw that, Emilia," the duchess called, not even glancing back. How…?

As soon as the duchess had gone, Emilia dissolved into laughter. "How does she manage that?" They'd long speculated that she'd been born with eyes in the back of her head.

"I've told you since we were children that she's part witch."

They shared another laugh. Barry glanced back at the door. "I should indicate that the Duchess of Sutton was not looking for Mother, and by my accounts, with her duchesslike, mincing steps, combined with the distance between your rooms and the music room, you've no more than twenty-five minutes to find yourself another hiding place."

A wave of gratitude swept through her, and she wished she hadn't been such a miserable elder sister to him when they were younger. Emilia offered him a grateful smile. "Thank you, Barry."

His cheeks flushed red, the same way they had when he was a boy who'd been caught in midprank. He held his hands aloft. "Lest you shatter my reputation as a bothersome brother, it's not purely altruism on my part. As long as she has a spinsterish-in-age daughter to worry about wedding off, she's far less concerned with her still-unwed ducal heir."

Emilia stuck her tongue out. "Oh, hush."

"What? I said 'spinsterish in age,' which is *vastly* different than calling you a spinster."

They shared a smile.

"Twenty-two minutes," he pointed out, lifting his timepiece.

"Thank you, Barry."

"Oh, and Emilia?" he said as he opened the door. She stared quizzically back. "If I might suggest, in the future you might consider choosing an altogether more reliable hiding place than your rooms." With a wink, her brother left.

The moment he'd gone, Emilia scrambled to gather up her book and two of the pencils her mother's thumping had scattered over the desk. Her belongings tucked in her arm, Emilia abandoned the guest chambers.

Using the servants' stairway, Emilia made her way down the darker, more narrow space until she reached the second level of the duke and duchess' sprawling manor house. The moment her slippers touched the plush crimson carpet, Emilia took off running.

Despite her parents' desire to see her married to, really, *anyone* at this point, Emilia had every intention of not only preserving her freedom, but also helping other young ladies to avoid making the same mistakes she had.

The problem with being a woman—of any station—was that the world, her parents included, had their own expectations about what said women wanted.

Emilia reached the end of the corridor and peeked around the corner.

Empty. She raced off once more.

Yes, everyone trusted they knew what a lady wanted:

A husband at eighteen.

A parcel of children to soon follow.

A career as Society's leading hostess.

Everything came down to marriage: Who would make one the best union? Which familial connections were most valuable? Would one settle for security or risk all on a love match?

What Emilia really wished for... was freedom.

That discovery had come compliments of the broken heart she'd suffered at the hands of a feckless cad. Her family, also Society, would not dare to believe her, because to all of them, all women invariably wished to marry. It was a lie perpetuated by the world, many women included.

Slowing her steps, Emilia crept down another one of the Duke and Duchess of Sutton's endless corridors.

Voices drifted from the intersecting corridor. Voices that grew increasingly closer—those of Lady Lauren Grace and Lady Ava Smith, two of Society's leading diamonds and nastiest gossips.

Oh, bloody hell. She abruptly stopped.

"They say Lord Whitworth ran off and married the first woman he could find."

Emilia's face pulled.

So *that* was what they were saying about the Duke and Duchess of Sutton's youngest son and his wife.

"Why ever would he do that?" Lady Lauren piped in.

Yes, it was, in fact, a fair question: Why would a notorious rogue rush off to marry... anyone?

Lady Ava lowered her voice to a still-loud whisper. "They said he did it so he couldn't be forced into marriage"—there was a pause—"with her."

Emilia froze.

"Lady Emilia Aberdeen?"

There it was.

"Of course, who else?"

Yes, who else? What other lady present for the gathering was almost thirty and lacking in suitors and seemingly reliant upon familial connections to make a match?

The pair of footfalls stopped.

"Well, that hardly makes sense." Lady Lauren, who'd ceded all superiority in the current discussion, spoke with far less confidence than before. "Why would they marry her to Lord Sheldon?"

"They wouldn't anymore, silly."

Emilia would have wagered her coveted freedom that Lady Ava had just given an impressive roll of her eyes.

"Because he's married now. But he was... *is* the lesser of the brothers."

Lesser?

Emilia furrowed her brow. And then it dawned.

"Ahh." Lady Ava's tones indicated she'd also quite caught on to her friend's thinking. "Lord Heath. Because he is—"

"A future duke," Emilia mouthed as the busybodies spoke in unison.

"A future duke."

Yes, because that was what every lady craved: marriage to a duke. Emilia stared blankly at the crimson silk paper adorning the wall across from her with faint spadelike shapes etched in gold. She traced one of those almost-hearts beside her.

Nay, that isn't what you craved. You wanted the heart of a duke. Altogether different, and yet, at the same time, not. Because Emilia should have, even then, known that those lords just a smidge below royalty weren't men to entrust one's heart to. They lived for their own pleasures and thought nothing of breaking hearts or even legal contracts, such as the betrothal the Duke of Renaud had severed.

Someday, I shall have the heart of a duke.

Giving her head a shake, she forced aside foolish thoughts of the cad from her past. It had been all the talk of marriage that had brought the memories back this night. She'd heard enough gossip from the pair.

"Yes, I have it on the authority of my mother that the Duke and Duchess of Sutton didn't wish to waste the ducal heir on a spinster." The ducal heir also happened to be the best friend of the man who'd stomped all over Emilia's heart. "Which quite means—"

Again, the girls spoke as one. "He is available."

And they were welcome to Lord Heath. Even when she'd been betrothed to Connell, his closest friend in the world had been as aloof as Lady Jersey welcoming a courtesan to her soiree. Distant. Always turning on his heel to make a hasty retreat. Increasingly so the closer she'd gotten to her wedding day.

How happy he must have been when his friend threw her over.

The miserable blighter.

"He is quite… handsome."

They dissolved into a fit of giggles.

Ah, giggles. The sounds of innocence and naïveté and childish dreams.

In fact, Emilia would have managed to feel a modicum of regret in knowing that these two would one day have their hearts crushed by life—if they hadn't already been horridly unkind.

Even with that, there was a sliver of sadness for the inevitable fate that awaited them. It awaited them all.

Emilia sighed.

"What was that?"

It took a moment to register that the giggles had faded, and then the footfalls resumed, coming closer. More quickly.

Bloody hell. Springing into movement, Emilia darted in the opposite direction, her skirts whipping around her ankles.

"…I saw," one of the gossips was saying, and by the direction of her voice, the young woman was at the corner. Oh, hell. "It was her skirts. I'm sure of it. The Ice Princess in her ice blue."

Heart racing, Emilia grabbed the nearest door handle. It gave way with a satisfying click. Relief flooded through her as she stumbled into the room and hurriedly closed the door behind her.

Safe.

And then she went absolutely still.

Oh, bloody hell.

Of all the three hundred and twenty-six rooms in the Duke and Duchess of Sutton's property, Emilia had chosen the one that was occupied.

By him.

Hovering over the billiards table, frozen midway through his shot. Sans jacket, no less.

Lord Heath Whitworth, the Marquess of Mulgrave.

By the horror settling on the angular planes of his face, the marquess looked about as pleased to see her as she was to see him.

For the briefest of moments, she considered taking her chances with the enemies on the other side of the door rather than with the enemy within.

After all, she and Heath had been anything but friendly toward each other... ever.

"...she was listening," Lady Lauren hissed from outside the billiards room. Or mayhap it was Lady Ava. With the high whine muffled by the panel, it was nigh impossible to sort out who was who.

In that moment, it was also settled—she chose the enemy within.

Emilia locked the door.

Pressing a finger to her lips, she urged a still motionless Lord Heath to silence.

"...in there," the other friend said. "Hello?" The impressively bold creature gave the door handle a jiggle.

Even knowing she'd turned that latch, she felt a brief moment of panic. Keeping close to the wall, Emilia inched slowly away from the door.

When it became clear that her hiding space was safe after all, some of the tension went out of her.

"We saw you eavesdropping," one of the gossips charged from the opposite side of the panel.

Her stomach sank. *Bloody hell.* They knew it was her. She was rubbish at this subterfuge stuff, after all. It wasn't her work for the *London Post* that would be her downfall, but rather, being caught sneaking about.

"I'll have you know," Lady Ava schooled, "it is *quite* bad form

listening in on two young women in the midst of a private discussion."

It took every last shred of restraint she'd mastered over the years
to keep from pointing out that private discussions were better off
not conducted in a hallway. Regardless, Emilia rather thought she
might have too hastily judged that particular gossip. Anyone bold
enough to call out a stranger, sight unseen, in a duke's household
had more gumption than she'd credited.

The girl jiggled the handle once more. "Show yourself."

From the corner of Emilia's eye, she saw Lord Heath motion to
her.

Hurriedly tugging his jacket from the chair resting at the sideboard, Lord Heath pointed in the direction of the door.

Emilia followed the gesture.

For one horrifying moment, she believed he was ordering her to
face the women on the other side.

With his right arm partially within the sleeve of his black evening coat, he impatiently jabbed his finger.

She widened her eyes. *The French Louis XVI three-fold giltwood
floor screen.* Collecting her skirts, Emilia darted behind the panels
just as one of the gossips tried the door handle again.

Then there was the faint whine of the door being opened. "May
I help you?" he asked in cool tones.

A long silence met the query. Emilia's heart pounded so loud she
was certain the two women could hear it.

One of the women broke the silence. "My lord," Lady Ava whispered with such an obsequiousness in her voice that Emilia rolled
her eyes. "We didn't... We believed..."

"I was listening in on your gossip?" he asked in icy tones.

"No..." the young woman was saying. "We were... That was...
mistaken," she squeaked. "We were mistaken."

Lord Heath's impressively frosty inflection must have been passed
on from duke to ducal heir. Lord Heath wielded it with the ease
of one who'd been born to this world knowing precisely what fate
one day awaited him. Had she ever before heard those tones from
Connell's best friend? She wrinkled her brow. For that matter, had
she even heard him speak more than a handful of sentences? He'd
always been in a haste to be free of her and Connell's company.
Granted, her own friends had been rightfully nauseated by Emilia

and her then–betrothed's fawning.

After a flurry of stammered goodbyes and no doubt deeply dipped curtsies from the women, Lord Heath closed the door and locked it once more, shutting Emilia in with him.

She remained hidden by the folding screen, her book clutched tightly to her chest, long after the pair had gone.

Waiting for an indication that it was safe to emerge from her hiding place.

Craack.

Emilia puzzled her brow.

Why… why… had the gentleman simply just resumed his game?

As if in confirmation of the wonderance, there came another *craack.*

Why… why… the bounder intended to play his damned game as if she weren't even there.

At last, after she'd been struggling with her latest column, inspiration struck.

Sinking to her haunches, Emilia opened her journal, and after tucking one of the pencils behind her ear, she began to write.

CHAPTER 3

If a gentleman treats you as though you are invisible,
you are better off with his disinterest.
Mrs. Matcher
A Lady's Guide to a Gentleman's Heart

HEATH RATHER SUSPECTED LADY EMILIA Aberdeen had no intention of emerging from behind that screen.

After three well-played strikes, he was rather certain of it.

Leaning over the velvet table, his arm drawn back, he briefly lifted his gaze in the direction of that screen and, for a longer moment, contemplated his escape.

The young woman who'd stalked the halls of Everleigh as if they were her own and dueled quite wittily with her mother and father at countless family gatherings, was not one he'd have taken to hide as a grown woman.

And yet, hiding she was.

Just then, rule four—or was it five?—on his mother's list intruded.

If Emilia does seem upset, it is your gentlemanly responsibility and duty to somehow cheer her up.

Heath tugged at his cravat. She wasn't *necessarily* upset. There could be any number of reasons she remained behind that screen. She could be... Or...

Bloody hell. Nay, there really wasn't any reason she'd be behind there other than ladylike upset. There had been the two angry harridans and the obvious fact that she was even now hiding behind that screen.

Damn it. Not for the first time, Heath lamented not having more of his brother's effortless ability to charm. "Are you awaiting permission?" Heath completed his next shot. "If so, you needn't."

There was a beat of silence.

And then...

"My lord?" she asked tentatively.

Had Lady Emilia ever been tentative? Some of his most vivid recollections of the lady were of her minxlike escapades of chasing after gypsies and legends on her family's estates, all the while doing so over her mother's lamentations and pleading. Time had changed her. "Permission," he repeated, eyeing his next shot. "To emerge."

"P-permission," she sputtered, still in her hiding place. "I do not..." As if she too realized the inherent silliness of debating that point from behind the folding screen, the young woman stepped out. With a toss of her honey-blonde curls, she scowled at him. "I do not *need* permission to emerge." Nonetheless, it did not escape his notice that she remained rooted alongside that screen.

"I didn't presume you did. I just couldn't account, however, for why you'd opted to stay there."

It was likely the pattern she'd displayed over the years of being anywhere... well, anywhere he wasn't.

Not that he could entirely blame her. There was the whole awkward matter of her broken betrothal to his best friend.

"Yes, well..." She gave another toss of her curls. "Seeing as how two gossips hunted down my—"

"Hiding spot?"

A pretty blush climbed her high cheekbones. "Whereabouts," she settled for. "I thought it would be prudent to not simply rush out and engage *you* in a discussion."

She'd managed to deliver two insults in that charge—one challenging his prudence and two with that slightly overemphasized word. Even being the recipient, Heath was hard-pressed to not appreciate the effortless retorts.

"Furthermore," she went on, stalking over with a peculiar brown leather book and a pair of pencils clutched close to her chest. "Opening the door could have proven disastrous."

Being caught alone with Lady Emilia Aberdeen? Yes, there

would have been a scandal there, indeed.

"Had you remained silent," she went on, "they would have eventually gone on their way, and neither of us would have risked discovery."

"Ah, yes. But then they would have gone on believing you had been listening in on their conversation." Heath returned his focus to the billiards table. Bringing his shot forward, he sent his white ball flying for another. They collided with a loud crack. "Which I trust is, in fact, what you were doing?" He straightened and glanced over in her direction once more.

The glow cast by the row of chandeliers overhead bathed her face in light and put her deepening blush on display. "I wasn't... *listening* in, per se." She wrinkled her nose. "Not *intentionally*." She shifted her book in her arms. "Rather, I was avoiding—" Her lips immediately formed a tight line as she considered the door.

He arched a brow. "My mother's festivities?" he ventured, staking out his next shot. "You are not alone on that score." Solitude had been that elusive gift he'd craved before his mother had stormed this space and given him his marching orders for the remainder of the house party. "I trust you'll find the halls now safe for you to—" He cut off abruptly, noting that he was in the midst of conducting a one-on-one conversation—with himself.

Brow puzzled, Heath looked up and started.

Lady Emilia was in the midst of setting the burden in her arms on the sideboard, and he blanched. By all intents and purposes, it appeared as if... "My God, you intend to... *stay*."

Connell's betrothed.

Nay, former betrothed, but really, it was all the same. Not only had she invaded his sanctuary, she'd laid a damned claim to it.

Her lips formed a small moue of displeasure. "You needn't sound so horrified about it."

He'd sounded horrified because he *was* horrified.

"You most certainly cannot stay here." He'd done his good deed where Emilia Aberdeen was concerned that night. Saving her from gossips surely counted for something. It was one thing assisting a young woman seeking to escape a pair of busybodies and unwanted gossip. It was an altogether different matter keeping company with that same woman. Alone. "You'll"—his mind worked—"miss the fun planned by my mother," he said.

"Charades?"

"You quite excelled at it as a girl." A memory flitted in of her crawling on all fours around his mother's parlor, one arm dangling from her nose as she trumpeted the great elephant's sound.

"Pass," she said cheerfully and then marched across the room with determined footsteps.

He followed her every movement. What in blazes was she doing now?

Emilia grabbed one of the lattice-backed chairs and proceeded to carry it over to his sideboard. "You see, no one would dare search for me here. It is, in fact, the last place I would be."

He stared on, feeling like an actor in the midst of a performance without the benefit of his lines—any of them.

"Now, you? You, on the other hand, they would expect to be here," she went on, moving the decanters and glasses off to the left side of the mahogany piece.

His mouth opened and closed several times. Not because the chit's reasoning was accurate—he'd been found by his mother not even thirty minutes ago—but rather, because... "Are you trying to tell me to *leave*?"

The minx paused in her task to glance back at him with a blindingly bright smile. "That would be splendid. Thank you." With that, she arranged her belongings into a makeshift desk... and promptly began writing.

Thoroughly dismissing him and completely forgetting about his presence. Assuming he'd leave.

The insolent chit.

Such had always been the way with Lady Emilia. A truth that rankled even more now.

If he were a proper gentleman—which he always was—then he'd do just that.

"What in blazes are you doing?"

He was fair certain that cursing in front of the lady he was tasked with "showing a good time" would not earn his mother's approval. But a gentleman had to draw the damned line somewhere.

"Writing," she offered distractedly, not raising her gaze from the page. Her fingers flew as she wrote... whatever it was that occupied her attention. "You needn't worry about me. I'll not bother you while you play your..." Not breaking with her task, she waved her spare hand at the air. "Game. In fact, you may go about doing so now. I'm just going to…"

The young woman had already forgotten him.

"As she always did," he muttered, alternating his focus between the minx, his billiards table, and the door.

"As I always did what?" She paused to glance back.

Heath's neck heated. Apparently, the lady hadn't been so engrossed that she'd failed to hear that. "I didn't…"

"You said, 'As she always did,' to which I ask, what do I always do?"

This *would* be the moment the spitfire paid him some notice. But then, in fairness, every exchange they'd had from childhood to this moment had occurred before someone else. Never alone.

"You misheard me. I said, surely you kid," he smoothly put forward, and when presented with having the too-clever chit ferret out his lies, he opted to be the one to retreat. After all, nothing good could come from them being alone here.

Heath returned his cue to the rack at the back of the room.

"Lady Emilia," he said, sketching a bow.

The chit didn't even look up.

"I'll leave you to your… pastimes." Which begged the question, what in blazes were her pastimes? More specifically—his gaze dipped to the small leather journal she scribbled so frantically upon—what in blazes was she writing so intently? He squinted.

His interloper glanced up.

Emilia narrowed her eyes and lay her arms in a protective shield over those pages, hiding the words written there. "My lord," she said impatiently. She did not, however, make any attempt to stand and dip a curtsy… as every last fawning lady who hoped for the title of future duchess did before he even fully entered a room.

Dropping another bow, Heath beat a hasty retreat and conceded the room to Lady Emilia.

The moment Lord Heath vacated his billiards room, Emilia gave her head a bemused shake.

Now, *that* had come to be the all-too-familiar and expected response from Lord Heath. All of it.

Coolly polite. More than faintly aloof. And then dashing off.

Such had been his ways since... well, *forever*. Since she'd been a girl and he an older boy who'd had neither patience nor a moment to spare for his mother's young goddaughter.

It was why she'd known that Lord Heath's desire to send her on her way moments ago hadn't been driven by any concern about her parents' sensibilities or a belief in her charades-playing skills.

Which she was rather masterful at.

That detail, however, was neither here nor there.

Emilia faced forward, determined to renew her work and reread the handful of sentences she'd written in response to the latest question from one of her readers.

If a gentleman treats you as though you are invisible, you are better off with his disinterest. But also, be reasonably suspicious of a gentleman who shows a fawning interest in you. A lady is best served to find a gentleman who wishes to be with her, but is not false in that desire.

Emilia paused midsentence and reread the words there. Words that came from a place of knowing. She'd no wish to be near *any* person who didn't genuinely desire her company. Gentlemen, like Lord Heath, with their effusive bows and hasty exits. She'd made fool enough of herself for one bounder. Her interests were now singular and fixed on helping other young women avoid the same missteps she herself had made.

And yet...

Unbidden, her gaze crept back to the door.

It was one thing to remember the lifetime of Lord Heath's icy disdain toward her. It was altogether different when he'd been the person who'd rescued her this night from certain humiliation at the feet of two societal gossips.

That defense, his opening the door and facing down the harpies, all to protect her had been... unexpected.

And made her think... Nay, it made her see that mayhap there was more to the gentleman, after all. Mayhap she'd misunderstood him, or unfairly judged him, or—

A small scrap of white snagged her notice.

Leaning down, Emilia peered at the page resting on the floor.

It was... a note.

Oh, bloody hell. This was certainly a test of her character and strength.

She forced herself to turn around to resume her work.

It is not your business. It is not your business. It is not…

Emilia tapped her pencil back and forth on her book, from top to bottom. From the corner of her eye, she peeked over at that forlorn scrap of white just lying near the billiard table. After all, any guest might come in and find it. That was, another, less reliable guest. A gossip. Someone who'd read that note and bandy its contents about to the Duke and Duchess of Sutton's other guests.

Yes, she couldn't very well leave the note there. In fact, she was the more reliable person to discover said scrap. Setting down her pencil, she stood and hurried over to gather up the note. Unbidden, her gaze skimmed the page.

Why… it was a list of some sort.

Emilia turned it over in her hands. The handwriting was familiar. How did she know that handwriting? How—?

Her eyes widened. "The Duchess of Sutton." She'd seen enough letters delivered from one duchess to the other to recognize it. She made to fold the page. After all, she couldn't very well go about reading her godmother's note.

Except…

Emilia chewed at her lower lip.

It wasn't truly a note. It was a list about…

Emilia's gaze dipped once more.

1. Inquire after her interests <u>and take part in those activities with her.</u>

Why… why… A little laugh built in her throat, and she clamped a palm over her mouth to stifle the revealing sound, lest she give herself away. The list was instructions, more than anything, advising the recipient on how to woo one of the guests. The Duchess of Sutton was playing matchmaker, and as her youngest son had already wed, it could only mean she sought to maneuver Lord Heath, her eldest and the ducal heir, into a match with an unnamed lady.

This time, she couldn't help it. Her laughter, pulled from her, more unrestrained and freeing than any other laugh she'd laughed these past ten years.

Emilia warred with herself. It was the height of rudeness to read another person's notes. Although… Emilia *was* Lady Sutton's goddaughter, and just as important, Emilia was London's most notorious columnist with matchmaking advice.

Why… it would be rude to not read the note and secretly offer help where she could to Lord Heath and his nameless lady.

2. She arises early for the morning meal. (Six o'clock punctually.) Break your fast with her.

Another young woman who rose at six o'clock. Splendid. As one who herself rose early and supped before most of the house had even begun to stir, it would certainly make it all the easier to identify the young lady's identity.

3. Be a good conversationalist to her. Express an interest in whatever subject she speaks to you on. Ask questions. Ladies like to know people care about what they are talking about.

It was generally good advice the duchess had written down for her son. And yet…

"Based on our last run-in, Lord Heath, you're going to require assistance with those instructions," she murmured and kept reading.

4. Do try to make her laugh. She's still hurting.

Emilia's heart tugged as all her earlier amusement fled. The woman had been hurt. It was a sentiment Emilia could identify with all too well. She sighed and hurried through the remainder of the duchess' list.

5. If she seems upset, it is your gentlemanly responsibility and duty to somehow cheer her up.

Lord Heath wouldn't know how. He'd be the last person who'd ever be capable of cheer, let alone cheering anyone up. Either way, the subject of this note was not unlike Emilia of years ago: an object of pity and well-meaning intentions by some and gossip by all. As such, this was not Emilia's business.

She made to refold the note when her gaze snagged on a heavily underlined and starred note:

Do ****<u>not</u>****, *under any circumstances, discuss her—*

Emilia stumbled, unable to vocalize the remaining two directives. *Do* ****<u>not</u>****, *under any circumstances, discuss her betrothal to that scoundrel you call friend.*

"It *is* my business," she breathed, her eyes immediately going back to that last item. Then, with something akin to horror, she reread the other familiar details about the mystery lady written upon the note.

Why… why… She gasped and dropped the page as if burned. *Why, why, I am the object to be pitied. She* was the one her godmother had ordered her son to see to.

The duchess wasn't matchmaking, she was coordinating events for the pitiable spinster. Which was—she cringed—somehow even worse than being the subject of a matchmaking.

The tightening in her chest was not a product of her memories of Connell.

Rather, Emilia's hurt came from the fact that the world would forever see her—and remember her—for how she'd been treated by that feckless cad.

Even her parents, her godparents, Polite Society, and, by the contents of this note, Lord Heath saw only her marital failings when they looked at her.

That item on his mother's list no doubt accounted for his earlier *rescue*. The gentleman who hadn't mustered more than a casual mention to her of the weather these past years had suddenly intervened on her behalf with the two gossips earlier? Now it at last made sense.

Well, they could all go hang. She hardly needed anyone to cheer her up or converse with her or rescue her or… or… "Anything I want," she whispered into the quiet. Her mind slowed and then resumed racing at a brisk clip. Hurriedly picking up the piece of paper, she reread the suddenly interesting again note. They'd all but handed Emilia that which she'd sought for this painful house party—an excuse to be away from her mother's matchmaking attempts and the other guests' gossip. For the first time since she'd discovered the letter, a genuine smile curled her lips.

Emilia returned the paper to its earlier place on the floor. Mayhap Lord Heath might be of service to her, after all.

CHAPTER 4

Never trust a rumpled gentleman. They are invariably
rogues, scoundrels, and cads to be avoided.
Mrs. Matcher
A Lady's Guide to a Gentleman's Heart

NEARLY TWENTY MINUTES LATER, SOMETIME between dismissing his valet and removing his cravat and jacket, Heath was besieged by the familiar feeling that he was forgetting something. The same sense he'd had the day his brother Lawrence had raced Sheldon and died, that something was wrong even before the world had been flipped upside down by grief.

Seated at the edge of his bed, with one boot removed and his fingers set to work on the other, he frowned.

What in blazes was it?

"No doubt it was your hasty flight from the minx," he mumbled under his breath, struggling with the boot.

After all, he'd left in such haste.

And yet—he paused again.

No, it was that sensation that occasionally came upon him. It had been there at the oddest times, oddly prophetic in its accuracy. The day his younger brother Lawrence had died. The moment Connell had sent 'round a note and then hightailed it from London, breaking his betrothal to Lady Emilia.

"You're being an arse," he muttered, giving his head a shake.

"Aside from seeing the young lady, nothing out of the ordinary is different…" His words trailed off. His heart hammered peculiarly. "The note," he whispered. Heath patted his chest and then searched for his jacket.

Shoving to his feet, he was across the room in three great strides. He grabbed the jacket and proceeded to fish around the inside of the silk lining.

Oh, bloody hell. His gut churned. It had to be here. It had to be here. "Be here. Be here. Be here." It proved a useless mantra.

Nothing.

Dropping to his knees, Heath crawled around the floor in search of that damned scrap.

Where was it? Where was it?

And bloody hell, why was there a damned Aubusson carpet with a bloody intricate pattern that obscured everything?

Dragging his hands along every corner of the floor, it took barely any time to discern that the list wasn't there.

Which could only mean… Somewhere between his unexpected meeting with Lady Emilia and his trek to his rooms, he'd lost it.

Oh, bloody, bloody hell.

Spinning on his heel, Heath took off running, racing the same path he'd taken earlier. Searching as he went. His gaze on the floor, he collided headfirst with a wall.

With a grunt, Heath staggered back, landing hard on his arse. Rubbing his head, he glowered up at his youngest—and entirely too amused—brother, Sheldon. Or Graham. Or whatever the hell he wanted to be called these days.

"You seem distracted," Sheldon drawled, holding a hand out.

Taking that offer, Heath jumped up, then registered his ever-vexing brother's attention on his feet. More specifically—

"You are barefoot."

His bare feet. Yes, his brother would notice as much. But then, no gentleman generally went around sans boots, particularly Heath. "Stockinged feet are hardly the same," Heath said defensively, dusting his palms over lapels… that weren't there.

"You are, uh… missing a jacket, brother," Sheldon pointed out, remarkably deadpan.

Heat splotched Heath's cheeks. He couldn't very well go about saying that he, the reliable son, had gone and lost a damned list given to him by their mother. A list pertaining to her goddaughter, and there was, in fact, a houseful of guests. His stomach dropped. *Dead. I am dead.* "There were…"

Sheldon quirked an eyebrow. "Yes?"

"Matters of import that I needed to attend to," he neatly substituted. Heath made to step around his brother, but Sheldon slid into his path, preventing that escape. Blast and damn. He didn't have time to stand here indulging his brother's humor. He clenched his jaw to keep from saying as much. Frantic worry over that missing list aside, Heath was the one who'd let his ducal guard slip, yet again, that night. "What is it, Sheldon?" he asked with remarkable calm.

"Given that you're half naked, I'd dare say whatever has you rushing around must be a matter of grave importance."

"It is of *some* importance." Grave. It was absolutely grave. He made another sidestep.

His vexing sibling proved tenacious, locking steps with him yet again. "How important?"

Grave had been correct. He'd sooner lop off his arm than admit as much to his younger brother, who by the glimmer in his eyes was enjoying Heath's circumstances entirely too much. "Important enough that I'd be better served elsewhere and not indulging your amusements here," he said, bowing his head slightly. This time, when Heath stepped around Sheldon, his brother made no attempt to block his escape.

He'd made it no farther than three strides before his brother called out. "I don't suppose this is what has you in such a frenzy?"

Heath spun back.

Leaning a lazy shoulder against the wall, Sheldon stood there with his arms folded and an all-too-familiar piece of vellum in his hands.

Any other time, he'd have been horrified that his scapegrace brother would be the one to find it. "Oh, bloody hell," he breathed, charging over to claim that hated scrap of paper.

"You're welcome," Sheldon drawled as Heath ripped it from his fingers. "You should have a care with that. Perilous stuff when information finds itself in the wrong hands."

Were there really any right hands, however, for that note? "Where did you find this?" he demanded, stuffing the scrap inside his—

Sheldon leaned forward. "This is where a jacket might prove helpful," he said in a conspiratorial whisper.

"Oh, go to hell," he muttered, and his brother laughed uproariously.

If he were one of those lords given to crudeness, this was certainly where Heath would begin turning a middle finger up at his younger sibling. "Where—?"

"You've my son to thank for discovering it."

His stomach plummeted. "Frederick?" Who else might have seen that damning page?

"Alas, there is only one son, for now. Fortunate for you, he asked me to join him in the billiards room a short while ago."

"The billiards room," he echoed, his eyes briefly sliding closed. There was a God, after all. Their mother's guests were still engaged in the evening's round of eternal charades, as he'd come to refer to it as a boy, and therefore, no one...

No one... that was...

Except...

Pass. You see, no one would dare search for me here. It is, in fact, the last place I would be...

Oh, blast and damn. His eyes flew open, and Heath grabbed his brother by his lapels. "The billiards room," he repeated, shaking him slightly. "Was there anyone else in there? A..." He glanced around quickly and spoke in a hushed whisper. "A..."

"Woman?" Sheldon neatly supplied. "As in the mysterious woman whom our mother was indiscreet enough to make a list about?" He waggled his eyebrows.

Damn his brother. He was having entirely too much fun with this. All of this. "Go to hell," he said again quickly, releasing him.

His brother's smile faded, taking all his earlier amusement with it. "There was no one there when we arrived. The note was just under the billiard table."

Where he'd been playing when Lady Emilia had arrived and upended his game... and from there, his whole damned night. Though, in fairness, his mother was more responsible than anyone else. "You are certain?" he pressed.

"Certain there was no woman? Or about the location of the note?"

Heath gave him a sharp look, earning a sigh.

"Oh, very well. I'm certain on both scores. You do know you're dreadfully straitlaced and becoming increasingly more so the older you get."

"I'm not straitlaced." He bristled. "I'm respectable. Honorable. Reliable."

Sheldon leaned over. "Yes, so reliable that you went about losing a confidential list."

And damn his younger brother for being correct... in this. He'd concede that and not an inch more. Heath glanced down at the object of all his woes this night, skimming it.

"Furthermore," Sheldon said while Heath read that page, "all jesting aside, though it is certainly unsettling to lose it, there's hardly anything identifying on it."

"Other than Mother's handwriting."

"There's that," Sheldon conceded. "Many of the guests who've been assembled, however, have been brought forward as marital prospects for you."

He winced. Yes, Heath had suspected as much. "But how many of those ladies break their fast at six o'clock?" he pressed, and his earlier panic returned.

His brother lifted his shoulders in a shrug. "My wife is also an early riser and dines before the other guests."

Fair enough.

In a rare show of support, Sheldon tossed an arm around his shoulders and squeezed. "No one discovered it. They could have. But they did not."

Breathing slowly between his teeth, Heath dusted a hand through his hair. Yes, having lost the note could have been calamitous, and yet, it had since been found... by his brother. It was an unfamiliar state for him to be in—making a misstep in front of... anyone. Heath found himself unnerved by the show of sibling solidarity.

"Mother really shouldn't have put anything to paper."

"Certainly not. But given that it was you, the ever-responsible, meticulous one," Sheldon said dryly, without inflection, "she probably trusted that any instruction she gave you, in any form, would be safe."

Yes, there was that. High expectations had been set not only by his parents but by every tutor who'd firmly instructed Heath on his responsibilities as ducal heir. Responsibilities that now included—he looked down at the note once more—entertaining Lady Emilia Aberdeen.

"Now, if I may suggest you seek out your rooms? By my estimation, the guests have another"—Sheldon consulted his timepiece—"twenty minutes or so of their evening's entertainments."

Folding the list into neat quadrants, Heath concentrated all his energies on that minute task. He attempted all the dignity one might muster after making a near-epic blunder. "Sheldon..."

"Graham," his brother slipped in.

"Yes, Graham, then." Defiant in everything, his younger brother had even claimed ownership of his middle name as his first. "I wanted to say..." He coughed into his fist. "That is... Thank—"

"You needn't even finish those words," his brother cut him off. "That is what brothers are for."

That is what brothers are for. It was an interesting statement and avowal from two boys who'd once been friends, but had drifted apart after the death of their other brother. Managing a grateful nod, Heath hurried back toward his rooms. After Lawrence's death racing Sheldon—*nay Graham*—every member of the Whitworth family had... been changed. And just as much, how they'd treated one another and behaved around one another... all that had changed, too. Lawrence's passing had served as a reminder to his then-young self how precarious life was and how much rested upon his shoulders. From that day on, he'd not made a single misstep. He'd not allowed himself to commit one. Rather, he'd conducted himself only in a respectable manner, carrying himself with dignity and—

"How... unexpected running into you again, Lord Heath... and in a state of dishabille, no less."

He stumbled a step.

Oh, bloody hell. God hated him. There was no other accounting for it.

For a long moment, Heath contemplated the path forward. He could very well simply pretend he'd not heard the minx. The minx with amusement heavy in her musical voice.

Except, he also had detected something else underlying Emilia Aberdeen's tone—a knowing. She believed that gentleman that he was, he'd do the gentlemanly thing and make a quick retreat. Given the respectable way in which he'd conducted himself since... the nursery, it was a likely conclusion for the lady to come to. And yet, it was also the reason he found himself turning around.

The golden-haired minx didn't so much as widen her eyes at the state of his dress. Or rather, undress. "Lord Heath," she murmured, with a deep curtsy.

He narrowed his eyes. He was believing that show of decorum from this woman even less than he was believing his father's prized horses would be flying over the damned walls of Everleigh. Nonetheless, he could play the game of pretend formality with the best of them. "Lady Emilia." Heath sketched an equally deep bow.

At the sight of one's host indecently clad, a doe-eyed debutante would have averted her eyes and taken off down the opposite hall. Lady Emilia, however, was no doe-eyed debutante. She was a woman grown now—and tenfold more impish than when she'd been a girl. She abandoned all earlier pretense of propriety and stared baldly at his feet.

"Sleep wandering."

He blinked and followed her stare downward, almost thinking he might find those words scrawled on the flooring. What in blazes was she...?

"Are you a sleep wanderer, my lord?"

Apparently, he was the only one of their unlikely pair to appreciate how utterly preposterous it was that she should *my lord* him. First, they'd known each other as children. And two, well, he was nearly unclad before her. "I trust we've moved into the realm of using one another's Christian names," Heath said with an impressive drawl his brother would have been hard-pressed to emulate.

"Very well. Are you a sleep wanderer, *Heath*?"

God, the chit was tenacious. "No, I'm not," he answered, folding his arms in a move that put the corner of the list in his hand on damning display. He swiftly jammed his hands behind his back.

Her too clever cornflower-blue eyes homed in on the hasty movement. Emilia took several steps closer. Drifting ever closer.

The insolent baggage.

She craned her neck so she might glance around his shoulder.

Heath hurriedly shifted, moving as she moved, rotating with her.

"Do you know, Lord Heath—?"

"Heath," he muttered inanely, his stomach muscles tightening. Who would have imagined that he'd have been better served to practice the art of subterfuge, after all? "The situation certainly seems to warrant the use of our Christian names." There was no escaping this. He'd wager all his future landholdings—entailed and unentailed—that the spitfire could have renegotiated the Lord Almighty into a second chance in that Garden of Eden had she so wished it.

Emilia stopped. So abruptly, he was knocked off-kilter, his back colliding with the wall. All earlier teasing was gone from the lady's tone and eyes, replaced by a sharpness in those deep blue depths. "I know what that is, *Heath*," she said evenly.

His stomach turned. "You do?" Heath again contemplated his retreat.

She leaned up. "Why, you have mail to post."

"Mail," he echoed dumbly. "At this—" He pressed his lips closed to keep from uttering the absurdity of posting mail at this late hour. Instead, he clung to the unexpected offering she'd held out. "You are correct.

She eyed him suspiciously.

And this was why he'd never bothered with the pranks his brother had. He was rot at it. Why couldn't he be more like Graham? It was not, however, the first time in his life that he'd wished for those skills. With his spare hand, he adjusted his cravat—that wasn't there—once more. "I've an urgent missive, and given the unpredictability of the weather we've been enjoying, I'd thought it prudent to have it sent. Immediately. Now." As if to draw further attention to the absolute ridiculousness of those ramblings, the longcase striking clock behind her marked the hour.

He winced as the Westminster chimes sounded over. And over.

Heath offered a sheepish smile through the clear ringing.

Remarkably controlled as she was, the lady returned that smile and waited until the ten whole beats had first played and faded before speaking again. "Is it a sweetheart?"

He stared blankly at her.

Emilia nudged her chin at him. "Your letter?"

Heath strangled on his swallow. "N-n-no," he said emphatically between his coughs. "Other business. It is *other* business," he settled for.

Emilia drifted closer, until she was a handbreadth away, the scent of her, apple blossom, unexpected and sweet, and he filled his lungs with that summer fragrance. "Is that your view of love and... *sweethearts*, Heath?" Emilia angled her face up toward his. "As formal business arrangements?"

He was still lost in that tantalizing fragrance, so it took a moment for her question to register. "No. I don..." Except... He frowned. The relationships he'd had in the course of his life, the lovers he'd taken, had all been neatly arranged formal affairs with contracts drafted. There'd not, however, been... a sweetheart. Such a relationship bespoke an intimacy greater than sex and was one he'd not known before.

An all-too-knowing smile danced on Emilia's lips. "I see." By the glimmer in her impish eyes, she'd declared herself the holder of his truth. Emilia stepped away, the scent of her lingering still. "I will leave you to your mail... Heath," she added, his name emerging as more of an afterthought than anything.

In fairness, that was what he had always been to her—an afterthought.

"Emilia." He straightened, bringing his shoulders back and his feet together. His damned stockinged feet.

Emilia's eyes dipped down toward the carpeted floor, and she lingered her gaze on his feet.

He resisted the urge to shift back and forth.

When she at last looked up, the familiarly teasing smile pulled at the corners of her lips. "Good evening, Heath."

"Emilia," he repeated for a second time, yet another reminder that he was not in possession of his roguish younger brother's charm or skill at discourse.

He waited until Emilia continued past, her curved hips sashaying, the ice-blue satin molding to a delicately rounded derriere.

Heath swallowed hard. *Do not look at her hips. Do not look at her—*

As if she'd heard that silent chastisement, she cast a glance back over her shoulder and, with a saucy wink, disappeared around the corner.

Fighting back a groan, he swiped a hand over his face—the hand with the blasted list that was the source of all his woes.

Damn his soul to hell.

Ogling his best friend's former betrothed, noticing the scent of her. Mayhap he had more of his brother's scoundrel blood in him, after all.

CHAPTER 5

The only worthy gentleman is the gentleman who'll
stand shoulder-to-shoulder with a lady.
Mrs. Matcher
A Lady's Guide to a Gentleman's Heart

IF EMILIA WERE BEING HONEST, she was rather enjoying her-self. More so than she had in the years since she'd been jilted. And certainly more than at any previous house party before.

And it was for the most unexpected of reasons.

Or rather, the most unexpected person.

Lord Heath Whitworth.

Nay…

Heath… The situation certainly seems to warrant the use of our Christian names.

Seated at the Duchess of Sutton's breakfast table, Emilia felt her lips tugging in a smile. And this was not a cynical or practiced or serene one she'd don for respectively appropriate moments. This was… a real one.

She'd forgotten what it was to truly smile, or tease, or do anything lighthearted. But now on two occasions—first, their meeting in the billiards room, and then in the corridor—she'd actually been enjoying her exchanges with Heath. During them, he'd not been the distant boy she'd known as a child or the aloof, proper ducal gentleman Connell called best friend.

Scribbling a small circle at the top of her page, Emilia peeked at the empty doorway and then over to the clock affixed along the front of the room. *Four past six.* Perhaps Heath was not coming. He'd only ever been punctual. Mayhap he'd no intention of fulfilling that list of obligations his mother had given him, a prospect that should bring with it relief.

It would mean Emilia needn't worry about a gentleman being underfoot or finding herself the object of self-pity. And she could devote her attentions to where they should be: on her advice column instead of on the list she now worked upon.

Her smile dipped as she stopped her distracted doodling.

What accounted for this peculiar *regret*, then? "You're being silly," she muttered.

"What was that, my lady?" One of the footmen hurried forward.

And now I'm talking to myself. "It is a bit chilly," she neatly substituted, making a show of adjusting her shawl.

One of the duchess' eager servants was already rushing over to the fireplace before she realized what he intended.

"No, you needn't. That is..."

The liveried servant set to stoking the fire over her protestations.

Stop it. Clear your head. She didn't require a gentleman about to enjoy herself. Why... why... her life had been quite full since Connell's betrayal. Abundantly so. Angrily flipping back in her book to the incomplete column for her editor, she resumed her work.

Do: Commit your future to a gentleman who allows you your interests and supports them. Each lady deserves a spouse who sees her value. Therefore, it is wisest to avoid those rakes, cads, and scoundrels whom Society sees as exciting.

Emilia paused in her writing and stared at that last sentence. As a rule, every lady, from debutante to dowager, craved the company of those thrilling *gentlemen.* She herself had been equally captivated by one such nobleman's charm. How different the Duke of Renaud had been than the staid, proper, respectable gentlemen. Gentlemen like Lord Heath Whitworth.

Except, stealing another glance at the clock, Emilia acknowledged that Lord Heath was not entirely—not at all—the pompous boor she'd taken him for. What else would she have thought about a boy who'd not played with her as a girl and then who'd been only aloof to her as a young woman?

Picking up her cup of warmed chocolate, Emilia flipped back to the note she'd made last evening about the gentleman now occupying her thoughts.

When she'd invaded his billiards room, he'd remained playing his game and then had faced her boldly—albeit sheepishly—when she'd discovered him unclad in the corridor.

These were unfamiliar sides to a man whom she'd seen, but not truly seen, before.

And you saw a whole lot more of him last evening.

Emilia devoted all her attentions to the contents of her cup, lest the pair of footmen at the opposite wall note the blush burning her cheeks. Emilia was no empty-headed ninny to go wide-eyed over a gentleman's physique, and yet...

Jacketless and in his bare, well, stocking clad feet. And she, for the first time in her life, had been... intrigued by Heath Whitworth, of all gentlemen. Tall, lean, and wiry, he'd an altogether different physique than her former betrothed. Only, sans jacket and cravat with his lawn shirt gaping open, she'd appreciated for the first time the chiseled perfection of his frame. From the aquiline nose, to the sharp cheeks, noble jaw, and brow, he put her in mind of one of those Greek statues she'd admired in the London Museum.

Unbidden, her gaze shifted to the doorway. Mayhap, she'd been wrong and Heath had no intention of dutifully following the items on his mother's list pertaining to the spinsterish houseguest.

Nay, he would.

Knowing him and his reputation as she did, she knew that he knew no other way. He'd be here.

And he'd fulfill every last item on that list.

She peeked at the clock. Six minutes past six.

Footfalls echoed in the corridor, tapping a purposeful, rhythmic march forward.

Her heart did a little leap, and she frantically flipped through her book to a clean page devoid of recriminating information.

When was the last time she'd been this excited about another person's company? It was only because of that list. That's all it was. Even saying that in her head, even telling herself that over and over, the lightness remained.

The footsteps stopped.

Her heart knocked harder against her rib cage, and she looked up from her book.

Taller than most men, he filled the entrance, looking—

Pained. He looked pained at being here, and she was certain she was going to hell for taking such delight in that. The bounder.

With all the ladylike lessons on decorum drilled into her, she glided to her feet. "My lord." Bowing her head slightly, she sank into a curtsy.

"Em—" He glanced to the servants at the sideboard. "Lady Emilia," he corrected, adherent to societal expectations. As he went to the sideboard to make himself a dish, she studied his broad back from under her lashes.

Neither servant made any attempt to make his plate for him, which indicated the gentleman saw to that task himself. It was a simple observation, and yet, as the daughter of a duke, she'd never before witnessed either of her parents undertaking the menial task. Once more, that also did not fit with the image she'd assembled in her mind of Lord Heath Whitworth. What else had she been wrong about where the gentleman was concerned?

After he'd made his plate, Heath carried it over to the table. She furrowed her brow. Or rather, he carried it *around* the table, taking the seat directly opposite her. Not even his mother's directives could compel him to take the seat beside her. No, that wouldn't be Lord Heath's way.

Emilia dropped her elbows on the table and craned her neck to better catch a glimpse of her only dining partner. Alas, the duchess' silver ewer, brimming with hothouse flowers sprigged with crimson holly berries, blocked her gaze. Setting aside her napkin, Emilia slid over to the empty place beside her. Leveraging her slippered foot on Lady Sutton's Swedish upholstered dining chair, she hoisted herself onto the edge of the table.

His jaw falling slack and his napkin fluttering in his fingers, Lord Heath angled his head… toward her, baldly watching her every move.

Emilia concealed a smile. Yes, the gentleman might be proper on the surface, but she was fast discovering there was a good deal more of him under that perfectly tailored black tailcoat. That was, a good deal more than the defined muscles of his chest. Reaching for the handle of the silver ewer, Emilia grabbed the arrangement.

She grunted.

The unexpectedly *heavy* arrangement.

Shimmying backward, she slowly climbed down from the table and landed on her feet. "There," she said cheerfully as she set the flowers at the head of the table. Emilia returned to her chair.

After she'd sat, Emilia dusted her hands together and claimed a now unobstructed view of Heath.

Heath, who sat there with that same dumbfounded expression on his face.

Snapping her napkin open, Emilia returned it to her lap, gathered her fork and knife—and waited.

"Would it not have been easier to ask one of the servants to move the item?" he asked, predictable with his question.

"Oh, undoubtedly," Emilia returned, slicing into a link of sausage. And waited—again.

Heath dragged his seat closer to the table. "And yet, you still climbed upon the table?"

He spoke like one trying to piece together the mystery of life. And since she'd lived a largely proper existence, her previous actions might as well have been one of those great mysteries. "And I still climbed on the table," Emilia needlessly confirmed, taking a bite of her sausage, enjoying herself immensely. More so than she had in—she searched her mind—*too* many years. This time, the wait stretched on. The gentleman she'd always known him to be would let the odd matter lie.

"Why?" The question came as if pulled painfully from him.

How much more she preferred this newer, more curious version of Lord Heath.

Emilia lifted one shoulder in a shrug. "It seemed the best way to illustrate a point."

"And what point would that be?"

"Just how outrageously silly it is that of all the seats"—Emilia waved the tip of her knife around the thirty-foot dining table— "in this whole room, you should pick *that* one." She jabbed the silver utensil at him. "Where we could not see one another." With that, she returned her focus to her breakfast plate.

Behind her, the pair of footmen stationed alongside the walls poorly disguised their laughter behind coughs.

There was a short pause, and then Heath slowly pushed back

his chair. Gathering up his plate, he came 'round the table and sat beside her.

She eyed his rather sparse plate dubiously. "*That* is your breakfast," she blurted.

Following her stare, Heath frowned. "What is wrong with my breakfast?" he asked, and she might as well have challenged his birthright for all the affront there.

Emilia smothered a laugh behind her hand. "I assure you, that is assuredly *not* breakfast."

"It certainly is." He reached for his napkin before seeming to realize he'd left it at his previous spot.

Emilia fetched him one from the empty place setting next to her and tossed it to him. Heath caught it in the air. "A single slice of unbuttered bread and one egg? These are not medieval times, Heath. Eating a proper breakfast isn't *praepropere*—"

"*Praepropere*," he silently mouthed.

"The sin of eating too soon, which is associated with gluttony," she clarified. "It is Catholic theological criticism."

Color splotched his chiseled cheeks. "I know what *praepropere* is."

"*Of course* you know," she whispered, leaning toward him.

His brows came together.

"Your plate, Heath." She sighed. "Your plate. The sin of gluttony. Your piousness."

"I'm not *pious*."

"Self-controlled, then," she allowed. Who could have imagined she'd have so much fun needling Heath Whitworth? Or that he'd be so very engaging?

"My eating a measured breakfast has nothing to do with my adhering to any ancient theologian rules."

"Splendid." She smiled widely. "Then let me help you." Gathering the various sweetcakes and pastries filling her plate, she proceeded to add the confectionaries and other offerings to his.

His mother's instructions rang clear in his head: Be polite, entertain the lady, and don't offend her. As such, with those orders doled out, Heath's life had become a farce.

There was nothing else for it.

How else to account for the fact that he now sat beside Lady

Emilia Aberdeen? Or the lady filling his breakfast plate with the items from her own?

When a second honey cake landed atop his ever-growing breakfast, Heath's patience snapped. "What in blazes are you doing?"

"I'm helping you," she explained, continuing to heap samplings from her dish onto his. "Thomas Wingfield wrote of the essentiality of breakfast. Thomas Cogan stated it was unhealthy to miss breakfast in the morning."

Thomas Wingfield? Thomas Cogan? "What in God's name are you going on about?"

With a beleaguered sigh, Emilia briefly paused in her undertaking. "Wingfield was a former MP from Sandwich. Cogan a medieval physician." She stared expectantly at him, and he, the bookish boy and then student he'd been and still was, hadn't a damned clue about either. "Either way," the lady went on as if further elucidating him on those figures was hopeless, "they strongly advocated against missing breakfast."

"I am not *missing* breakfast," he muttered as she moved almost all the items on her dish to his. "I was eating a measured one." Or he'd been attempting to.

Emilia added a brioche to his dish—his already filled dish. "Cogan was one of the first to claim that it was healthy for those who were not young or ill or an elder to eat breakfast." Widening her eyes, she glanced up.

Suspicion filled him. *Do not fall for that bait. Do not fall for that bait.* "What?"

"Well, it's simply that you're not young or ill, and so you must be…" She waved in his direction.

By God, the chit wasn't insinuating what he thought she was? "What?" he repeated, clipping out that single syllable.

"Well, an *elder*," she whispered.

The fork slipped from his fingers, and the metal clattered noisily upon the edge of his overflowing plate. "I most certainly am *not* old," he barked, and damned if his two disloyal footmen didn't dissolve into another round of pathetically concealed hilarity.

Emilia patted his hand. "Then your morning fast should reflect as much." She beamed, before returning to dicing up the same link of sausage she'd been nibbling since he'd sat across from her.

First the flowers, then her talk of old men and breakfast. The clever chit had steered him into a trap, and he'd fallen right into it… again.

"I'll have you know," he said gruffly, placing the white linen napkin upon his lap, "there is nothing wrong with my repast."

"No," she concurred, not even glancing up from her dish. Popping a bite of sausage into her mouth, she smiled at Heath. "Not anymore." She winked. "You are welcome."

The saucy chit.

Heath didn't know if he was entranced or incensed by the clever minx.

Entranced…?

Heath went absolutely still.

Entranced over Emilia Aberdeen? Nay, it couldn't be. It was impossible and… Well, no. It was just impossible. She was, and would forever be, Renaud's former betrothed. Admiring her in any way was strictly off-limits.

Not for the first time, annoyance with his mother and her damned list and what she asked of him settled in his chest. It was why he welcomed the unexpected quiet and calm between them as Emilia dined on the sparse contents of her plate.

Silence.

Be a good conversationalist to her. Express an interest in whatever subject she speaks to you on. Ask questions. Ladies like to know people care about what they are talking about.

Damn it to hell.

"You enjoy medieval studies." There, it was a fact she'd revealed… *And one you were intrigued by since the lady opened her plump, bee-stung lips.*

From the corner of his eye, he watched Emilia dab at the corners of that crimson flesh.

Oh, blast. Heath yanked his gaze away, diverting it toward the ceiling. His plate. The window. *Anywhere* but at that mouth he had no right admiring or appreciating. Or imagining the feel of under his own. *I'm going to hell.* Ironically, it was a task handed him by his mother that would send him there.

"I'm sorry?"

Had there not been a question tacked on the end there, he'd have imagined he was the one who'd spoken those words aloud. *Focus on your task and being a good conversationalist to the lady's inter-*

ests. "Medieval studies. I take it by the earlier edification you gave me that you enjoy medieval studies." It was both peculiar and intriguing.

She shrugged. "I enjoy all manners of different studies and topics."

With that, Emilia returned her focus to the plum cake on her porcelain dish. She proceeded to cut herself a small piece.

With her terseness, the lady wasn't making the task easy for him.

And yet, seated beside this minx who'd climbed atop the table and then prattled on about the origins of breakfast, he found he wanted to know more about that statement that offered everything and, at the same time, nothing about her interests. Nor was it any sense of obligation or promise he'd made to his mother, but more a genuine, far more dangerous need to know. "How does a young woman come to know about Cogan and Wingfield?"

Resting her elbow on the table, Emilia dropped her chin atop her open palm and turned her head to look at him. "Given they are deceased, I trust the same way a man comes to know about them." Her lips twitched. "From a book."

"You are a bluestocking?" he asked, that not at all fitting with the young girl who'd been more interested in flitting around the fair in her family's village than in the library to which Heath had opted to escape.

"No," she said simply. "I'm just a woman who likes to read and happens to recall certain obscure details and information." Emilia's lips formed a soft, knowing smile. That luscious flesh all but gleamed, the bright red hue giving the illusion that she'd painted them in a crimson rouge. It was an illusion, wasn't it? And God rot his soul for wanting to find out. "I know what you're thinking," she said.

"Impossible," he said hoarsely. *Oh, God, please let it be impossible.*

"You're thinking back to the younger girl who went out of her way to bother you."

Her matter-of-fact statement slashed across his lustful musings. Was that what she'd believed? "You never bothered me," he said quietly. He'd been endlessly fascinated by the whirlwind of life she'd been. He'd been unsure how to be around her, but she'd never been a bother.

She rolled her eyes. "Ever the gentleman you are, Heathcliff

Whitworth." Emilia rested her palms on the arms of her chair. "But you would be correct."

He didn't blink for several moments. That admission hardly seemed like one this woman would ever make to anyone, *especially* to him. "I am?"

"I wasn't a particularly bookish girl." Just like that, the light went out of her eyes, and he wanted the glimmer to spark once more. So he could see her as she'd been moments ago, teasing and merry.

Emilia's gaze fell to her breakfast.

She was hurting.

Damn it. And damn Renaud for hurting her, even as his reasons for jilting the lady hadn't been wholly dishonorable.

And damn me for not being the charming one capable of chasing away her sadness.

"Do you sketch?" he blurted, glancing to the book she'd been carrying around last evening.

Confusion brimming in her clear gaze, Emilia looked at him. "Do I...?"

Heath gestured to her book. "Sketch?" he repeated, drawing invisible lines in the air with his finger.

"Uh... no." Emilia followed his stare to the leather book beside her. "Yes. That is, *sometimes.*"

Oh, now this was an interesting reversal of roles. He'd managed to turn Emilia Aberdeen upside down. "Is it yes?" he drawled, finding a devilish pleasure in this unexpected turn. It was a welcome one. He grinned. For him, anyway. "No? Or sometimes?"

A pretty blush bathed Emilia's skin in a delicate pink. "All of them," she said quickly.

"Not at the same time, I trust?"

"Sometimes." As if realizing her blunder, the lady bit her lower lip, that row of even, pearl-white teeth worrying the flesh.

Hers was a siren's mouth that tempted. And just like that, he was knocked off-kilter once more. *Yes, I'm going to hell.* He briefly closed his eyes. *She is your mother's goddaughter. And more... worse, Connell's love.* Granted, his friend had ended the betrothal, but Heath was the sole person who knew the reasons for the decision that had not really been a choice. As such, imagining the wickedest pleasures for and with his friend's beloved's mouth crossed a line he'd never dare venture over.

"It is a list," Emilia finally murmured.

The casualness of her tone cut through his maddening thoughts. "What manner of list?"

First his mother's and now hers.

"Of activities." Warming to their discussion, she shifted closer. "I am compiling a list of activities I might see to that would occupy me during the remainder of the festivities."

This was safe. An opportunity to put some distance between them.

"My mother has organized activities for each day," he ventured in a coward's bid to save himself from a path of temptation he had no wish to wander down.

"This is a different list," she said with a wave of her hand.

"Yes, I see that," he muttered. "May I?"

Her already impossibly wide eyes formed perfect circles. "May you?" she squeaked, dragging the book close to her chest like a protective mama.

He sharpened his gaze on the small leather journal. Whatever was contained upon those pages was of great import. It was why she had that book in hand at nearly every run-in he had with her. It was why she even now clutched it close. Intrigue stirred.

Emilia followed his stare and then loosened her grip. "Uh…" She cleared her throat. "That is, you may." She proceeded to meticulously tear a page from the revered book and handed it over.

This was what was contained upon those pages? "Another list," he said under his breath.

"What was that, Heath?"

"Ice skating," he stated, reading item one on her list. "I was reading your item one aloud."

Emilia toyed with the edge of her book. "Sadly, I never learned how to ice skate." There was a faint trace of regret underlining the acknowledgment that he'd have to be deaf to fail to hear. "Daughters of dukes do not ice skate." She spoke in the rote manner of one reciting an all-too-familiar phrase. One that had no doubt been delivered countless times by her parents. She gave a wistful smile. "And because of that? I did not skate."

"How odd." The words left him before he could call them back.

The lady sat upright, and the soft, lost-in-thought set to her features faded. "You find it peculiar that I don't skate."

"I never expected that you…" Heath searched for the right

words that would not offend, reminded yet again of how he'd never managed them with the ease of Graham's or Emilia's former betrothed, Renaud.

"You never expected what?" She cocked her head. "That I bowed to Society's constraints?" she said, unerringly reading his thoughts.

"Precisely. I remember you as the girl who talked circles around your father until he agreed to allow the gypsies to stay on his property and return each summer for the annual village fair."

Surprise lit her eyes. "You remember that?"

His fingers twitched with the need to give his cravat a tug, and he resisted the telltale gesture of his unease. "I do."

Emilia leaned closer. "But that is just it, Heath," she whispered, her hushed words spoken in that faintly musical tone, quiet enough that they belonged only to him. "For every way in which I managed a show of defiance, there were ten other ways in which I was ever the dutiful daughter." Her face pulled. "Ply my needle, while Barry or Father read aloud from books that I despised. All the while, I perfected it all: drawn work, pulled-fabric work, stump work, stuffed work, cording, quilting, candlewicking."

His mind spun at that accounting.

"I venture you've neither heard nor practiced each of those stitches?" she asked, and this time as she smiled, it dimpled her right cheek.

He met her eyes and held her gaze, riveted, unable to look away.

"I've not." To give his fingers something to do, he reached for his cup of coffee, but Emilia caught his hand, staying the movement.

At the heat of her touch, he felt his heart go into a double-time rhythm.

"Which is precisely my point, Heath," she said without missing a beat, so matter-of-fact, wholly unaware of his increasingly acute awareness of *her*. "I learned all those pursuits expected of me just so that I might justify why I should then be able to engage in activities that truly interested me. And so there was much I missed out upon."

Heath had only ever taken Lady Emilia Aberdeen as one who'd proudly turned her nose up at Society's constraints. She'd been free, where he'd been trapped by his responsibilities as the ducal heir. Or so he'd believed. Now he stared at the woman beside him, seeing her in a new light. Seeing her in ways he never had before. Finding that she, *too*, had been limited by Society's constraints. *Just as you yourself were... and still are.* Heath worked his gaze over her face. "You may have honored those expectations, but you were also compelled to find your own interests and pleasures. And I?" A sad smile curved his lips. "I was ever the dutiful son mastering the names of Whitworth ancestors and reciting their accomplishments in Latin." God, he'd hated Latin.

Emilia started.

"What is it?"

"It is just that..."

Heath stared at her expectantly. "You thought that I enjoyed each lesson I received or every responsibility handed down?" he predicted.

The pretty blush staining her cheeks indicated he'd hit the nail on the mark.

"Some of it I enjoyed. Some of it I did not. But where you asserted some control over those expectations of you, I dutifully accepted each lesson and responsibility as my lot." Heath took a long swallow of his coffee. "And that, Emilia, is why you were different"—and braver and more interesting—"than my..." His lips twisted in a self-deprecating smile. "How did you phrase it? Pious self."

"I was teasing," she said softly, an apology there.

Heath waved it off. "I know." He'd only ever been treated with deference by everyone. Even his brothers had come to treat him differently. *Not Renaud, the man who'd intended to marry the woman beside you,* a voice needled at the back of his mind. And selfish bastard that Heath was, he forcibly shoved aside thoughts of his friend. "But you were not incorrect. I have lived a proper, staid life."

"There is nothing wrong with proper or staid."

He snorted.

"There *isn't*," she insisted, with such conviction that he almost believed her. "There is something comforting in it, even."

Heath stiffened. Did Emilia realize even now that she spoke in veiled tones of the man who'd broken her heart?

Emilia went silent and rested her palm on his, once more. She glanced down at their linked hands. A charged energy crackled between them.

Heath's heart knocked hard against his rib cage.

The feel of her hand on his and the warmth of that joining felt... right.

She was the first to break the connection. "Either way, given all that, you, too, know what it is to miss out on the fun of ice skating."

Heath frowned. "Why do you assume I don't know how to skate?"

She furrowed her brow. "Because, well..."

Because of who he was. Suddenly, the opinion she had of him grated. He might be a ducal heir, but blast and damn... he could have fun, too. Or he used to enjoy himself. "I assure you, I know how to ice skate." At least, he didn't believe a man forgot those skills. Surely it came as easy as riding?

Her eyes rounded. "You do?"

"Quite well." There'd been a time when he'd even outdistanced his younger brother, the more athletic Graham.

"That is splendid!" The mischievous glimmer danced in her eyes and set off warning bells in his head. "It is decided."

"What is decided?" he asked, straightening in his chair, already knowing he'd fallen into yet *another* damned trap.

Emilia plucked her brief list from the table. "I'll need twenty minutes." She shoved her chair back and, gathering up her book, started for the door.

"What is decided?" he repeated. "Twenty minutes for what?" he called after her, dread creeping in.

Spinning back, Emilia gave her eyes a roll. "Ice skating lessons." Her face fell. "Never mind. You needn't—" Her mouth trembled.

Heath held his palms up, warding off the evidence of her misery. "Good God, what is wrong with your lip? It's quivering. You aren't going to"—horror strangled his voice—"*cry?*"

"N-no." Emilia blinked wildly, and a single drop streaked down her cheek.

Ask her what she'd like to spend her morn doing, and then do it. And what was the other? Do not upset the lady.

Only, from their two exchanges and now dining together, he acknowledged a truth he'd not fully considered until now: Spending time with Emilia Aberdeen could only be perilous, for a whole host of reasons, not the least of which being his transfixion on her siren's mouth.

He swallowed a groan. "Very well. I'll accompany you. Twenty minutes."

"Splendid," she replied, clapping her hands once. "I'll meet you in the foyer shortly."

As she sailed from the room, Heath narrowed his eyes. Why, that show had been just that... a show. A carefully crafted display to secure his company.

The minx had bested him again.

CHAPTER 6

A lady should only give her heart to a man she enjoys being with and who brings her joy.
Mrs. Matcher
A Lady's Guide to a Gentleman's Heart

"YOU ARE SHAMEFUL. PATHETIC. WITLESS." The accusations spilled from Emilia's lips, and she stabbed a finger at her own guilty reflection in the bevel mirror. "And weak. You are weak, too. You were most certainly *not* supposed to enjoy yourself."

Emilia let her arm fall to her side.

And yet... she *had* enjoyed herself.

She swiped her bonnet from the dressing table and jammed it atop her head. "And with a gentleman who wants nothing to do with you," she muttered. Wasn't that always her way?

Everything about her exchange with Heath had been unexpected. Why, the gentleman she'd taken him to be would have been suitably horrified at having a guest—and a lady at that—climb atop the breakfast table and reposition his mother's floral arrangement. Instead, he'd met her challenge by collecting his plate and joining her at the opposite side of the table.

Emilia slowly looped the end of one velvet bonnet ribbon over the other. She'd set out to teach Lord Heath—*Heath*—a lesson, and at some point between last night and their time together in the breakfast room, she'd found that she rather liked being with him. She recoiled. There it was.

The pieces she'd taken as fact—his pompousness, his inability to jest, his unwillingness to have her around as a girl—had all proven erroneous on her part. The serious little boy she recalled, tucked away in his lessons while all the other children had played on his family's grounds, had proven capable of levity, after all. What was more disconcerting was the truth that they'd not been unalike growing up. They were, in fact, more alike than she'd ever credited.

Some of it I enjoyed. Some of it I did not. But where you asserted some control over those expectations of you, I dutifully accepted each lesson and responsibility as my lot.

Heath, however, did not see it that way.

I remember you as the girl who talked circles around your father until he agreed to allow the gypsies to stay on his property and return each summer for the annual village fair.

He saw them as different because of her few moments of rebellion and her willingness to challenge her parents. Emilia, however, was not deserving of that praise. For in reality, they had been the same in those regards—ducal children who'd bowed to the expectations placed upon them.

Emilia finished tying off her bonnet.

She found herself enjoying someone who understood what being the child of one of those exalted figures had been—and was still—like.

Even if he was a gentleman who'd avoided her through the years and paid her attention now only at his mother's bequest.

Suddenly looking forward to Lady Sutton's house party, Emilia gathered her red velvet cloak and tossed it around her shoulders. Humming the cheerful, upbeat melody of "I Saw Three Ships," Emilia next collected her leather gloves and started from her room. There was still a welcoming quiet in the halls while the other guests slept on. Part of the reason she'd taken to waking early each morn was so she could be assured she wouldn't be bothered by gossips—her mother included. The early hours so hated by the *ton* belonged solely to Emilia.

Only... not all the *ton* were late to rise.

Heath was also awake.

That is because his mother ordered him awake and in the breakfast room, you nitwit.

She'd do well to remember that. All of this, any time they spent together, was a pretense. He was the dutiful son cheering up the brokenhearted spinster.

Strengthened by that reminder, Emilia hurried the remainder of the way until she neared the top of the stairwell, where voices drifted toward her.

"Is this where you want it?" Heath's question was met with a child's giggle.

"You are being silly. If it is there, no one will walk under it, Heath."

"Being complicit in mischief I trust qualifies me to be called Uncle Heath," he drawled.

Intrigued, Emilia drifted closer and then hovered at the top of the stairway. Two pairs of skates lay forgotten at the bottom step. Emilia inched closer, and hugging the wall, she stared at the unlikely trio below.

Already wearing his cloak and Oxonian hat, Heath stood with a bough of yellowish flowers and white berries.

Near an age of ten or eleven, a pair of girls stared expectantly at him. "You are being deliberately evasive, Uncle Heath," one of the dark-haired girls said flatly. She jabbed a finger at the doorway. "There," she directed, like a military commander at battle.

The little group looked as one at the area in question.

Her curiosity redoubled, and Emilia angled her head to better see the reason for Heath's debate with his nieces.

"If you would, hang it there, please," one of the children urged.

The slightly smaller of the pair sighed. "Yes, hang it there and be done with it already."

"The front doorway. Uh… I trust that is… too obvious." He gentled the rejection with a smile.

"That is the point of mistletoe," one of the girls said with a toss of her head. "For people to find themselves caught under it." She grunted as her sister jammed an elbow into her side.

"It is a silly tradition, Creda."

"Silly? Silly is Uncle Heath attempting to affix it atop a mirror against a wall where no one will see it or walk under it."

He frowned. "Beg pardon," he said, with such a wounded expression that Emilia felt a smile tug her lips up.

The quarreling pair of sisters promptly ignored him. "If you find it silly, Iris, then you needn't be here." Creda gave a dismissive clap of her hands. "Where were we, Uncle Heath?"

Both girls stared expectantly at him.

"I was suggesting that we hang the ball—"

"The mistletoe," Creda supplied for him.

"Here." Heath hung the looped ribbon around the ornate work of a gilded mirror affixed to the wall.

Iris abandoned her negligent repose. "Well, who in blazes is going to walk under *that*?" she demanded, holding her palms up. "I mean, how would that even work? Would a person who looked in the mirror have to kiss their own reflection?"

"I... I..." He looked pained, and despite the particular glee she'd found in the whole endearing exchange, Emilia took mercy. She stepped out from the shadows and resumed her descent.

"Might I suggest a compromise?" she called down.

Three sets of eyes went whipping up.

Heath's eyes lit, and she paused at the unexpectedness of that response. Heath, whose gaze had only ever been averted or aloof when she was near. Only... no... there could be no mistaking that unexpected light there because of... her. A little fluttering started low in her belly.

Silly. He is simply grateful for your intervention. That compelled her forward. Emilia reached the bottom of the staircase and stopped. "Hullo," she greeted the twins.

"You are Lady Emilia, are you not?" Creda pressed, skipping over polite greetings.

It appeared Emilia's name was infamous even with children. "I am," she confirmed, turning her attention to the young girl.

Creda beamed. "Splendid! My mother speaks quite highly of you." With that avowal, she darted over to her uncle's side, snatched the bough from his fingers, and dashed back to Emilia.

"I believe this is where I'm doubly offended," he muttered.

Emilia's shoulders shook with silent mirth. "I trust you are searching for the ideal location for your mistletoe?" she asked, accepting the small holiday arrangement by the crimson ribbon. "The splendid thing about Lady Sutton's..." She paused. These girls had recently become stepgrandchildren to the hostess. "Your grandmother's household," she neatly corrected, "is that there are clever little nooks and adornments where one can hang all manner of"—she winked—"anything."

"Uncle Heath has spoken quite adamantly against the front doorway."

"As much as it pains me to agree with Lord Heath, I must confess the front doorway is not the ideal location for mistletoe."

Previously disengaged in the process, Iris, a shoulder propped against the wall, called over, "And why ever not?"

"Well, you see," Emilia went on, moving deeper into the massive foyer, "*everyone* walks through the front doors, oftentimes in groups. Mothers and sons and fathers and daughters. Brothers and sisters."

Both girls' faces pulled in a grimace. "Kissing one's brother?" they spoke in unison.

"I can see how I may have been incorrect about the placement, then," Creda mumbled.

Emilia's lips again twitched. "My point is not 'who' one"—she stole a glance from the corner of her eye at Heath—"meets under the mistletoe." Her cheeks warmed. "But rather, the unexpectedness of that... that... meeting."

"That kiss," Iris said, rolling her eyes.

For one wistful moment, Emilia envied the girl her youth and innocence. It had been a lifetime since she herself had been that forthright. "Correct. The kiss," she made herself say. "Not knowing who will find themselves under that doorjamb, at a given moment, accounts for the true excitement around the tradition."

Both girls went silent as they seemed to be thinking on it.

Over the tops of their heads, Emilia and Heath shared a smile.

"Thank you," he mouthed, touching a gloved palm to his chest.

Emilia gave her head an imperceptible shake, waving off the gratitude.

"Hmm," Creda said, more to herself. "Very well. You have earned the rights."

"The rights?" Emilia looked around at the assembled group.

Iris released an exaggerated sigh. "To select the placement." She pointed to the Duke of Sutton's leather library footstool.

"I've been stripped of my responsibilities, it would seem," Heath said dryly.

Emilia bowed her head. "I am honored." Doing a small circle, she took in the many options. She considered the arched entryways, parallel to one another. "Hmm." She tapped a fingertip against her lip and then abruptly stopped. "I have it!"

Emilia and the twins looked to Heath, who still stood there with his arms folded at his chest, and he let his arms fall to his sides.

"The *footstool*, Uncle Heath," Creda reminded in beleaguered tones.

Immediately springing into action, the marquess fetched the object in question.

"Over there, if you please." Emilia pointed to the selected entryway, and as Heath carried the requested object over to the indicated spot, a memory trickled in of herself, near in age to Creda and Iris, sitting and giggling with her friends Aldora and Constance around a worktable at Lady Sutton's. They were making garland and holly for the holiday party much the way these two little girls before her now did. Except...

Emilia frowned as another buried memory slipped forward.

"Do not look now, but Heath is in the doorway, Emilia," Constance said from the corner of her mouth.

She glanced up and caught Lord Heath peeking from behind the doorframe, his somber stare on the revelries.

He'd slipped away, and just like that, she and her friends had continued on. She'd never given a thought to why he'd been there. Now, as a grown woman who'd heard him speak of the rigid existence he'd known as a duke's son, she saw a possibility she'd not considered at the time—he'd wanted to take part in those festivities with the other children. A pang struck her chest.

"Lady Emilia?" one of the girls was saying, bringing Emilia back to the present.

"Hmm?" She blinked. "Oh, yes, uh... perfect," she said, hurrying over to Heath. He held a hand out.

Emilia stared at his long fingers cased in fine Italian leather gloves. "What are you doing?" she blurted.

His palm faltered. "Offering you a hand up?" His was a question.

"It is the gentlemanly thing to do." Iris imparted that advice like a seasoned finishing school instructor.

Except... it wasn't *the* gentlemanly thing to do. Gentlemen took on such tasks themselves, so as to ensure a lady wasn't injured. Or that was what her former betrothed had said when they'd decorated her family's townhouse the winter before they were to marry. As a young woman, she'd secretly chafed at his protective-ness, despising that he'd treated her like a cherished "object" to be guarded and not as a woman capable of hanging her own blasted mistletoe.

"Unless you'd rather I see to it?" Heath ventured.

"No," she said quickly. "I have it. That is…" She brought her shoulders back. "I'll see to it." Resuming her supervisory role, Creda returned to the middle of the foyer. Emilia accepted Heath's hand. "Do you know, the traditions around mistletoe go back thousands of years?"

Iris, who'd retreated to her place alongside the wall, straightened. "Really?"

"Really." Emilia nodded. "In fact, Roman naturalist, Pliny the Elder, noted it could be used as a balm against epilepsy, ulcers, and poisons."

Both sisters dissolved into another fit of giggling. "Holidays and poisonings are generally not two ideas that go together," Creda said, smothering her mirth with her palm.

"That would depend. Some might prefer a poisoning to one of my parents' house parties," Heath said under his breath, startling a laugh from Emilia. She promptly missed a step.

Heath shot an arm out and immediately caught her around the waist, drawing her close.

The laughter froze on her lips, and she went absolutely still in his arms. One might underestimate the strength of this slender and wiry gentleman—as she herself had done before this moment—and yet, pressed together as they were, she felt every contour of his biceps and rock-hard stomach. Emilia's mouth went dry as she lifted her gaze—

To Heath's concerned one. "Are you all right?"

No. I'm not. She was ogling Heath Whitworth. Emilia stole a peek from the corner of her eye and found Creda and Iris lined up beside them. Worse, she was ogling him in front of his young nieces, no less. "Fine," she squeaked. "I am fine." My God, when was the last time she'd squeaked? She was no debutante but an almost thirty-year-old spinster. "I stumbled." She stated the obvious for the trio staring back at her. *What had they been talking about? Think. Think.* The history of the mistletoe. Devoting her attentions to her task at hand, she climbed the last step. "The Greeks were also known to use mistletoe for menstrual cramps." As Heath strangled on his swallow, Emilia schooled her features, hiding the perverse glee she found in teasing the straitlaced lord.

"Menstrual cramps, you say?" Iris asked, meandering to the middle of the foyer and taking up a spot alongside her sister. "I'd like to know more about th—"

"The Romans viewed it as a symbol of peace and friendship." Heath spoke so quickly, his words rolled together as he effectively silenced the remainder of Creda's request with a recitation that likely came verbatim from a textbook. "According to legend, enemies who met under mistletoe would lay down their weapons and embrace."

His off-topic telling was met with several awkward beats of silence.

"I find I preferred Lady Emilia's more interesting talk on monthly courses," Iris muttered under her breath.

An endearing blush splotched Heath's cheeks.

Despite her resolve, Emilia shook with amusement.

"I am so glad you find this amusing," he said from the corner of his mouth.

"*Very* amusing," she whispered. Alas, she took pity once more. "Perhaps we can meet later and speak all about mistletoe and menses when Lord Heath is not about." She dropped her voice to a less-than-conspiratorial whisper. "You know how squeamish gentlemen can be."

"Are," Iris corrected, looking pointedly at Heath. "How squeamish gentlemen *are*."

Winking in agreement with that opinion, Emilia returned to hanging the mistletoe. Stretching up on her tiptoes, she draped the red ribbon over the curved ornamentation at the center of the entryway. "There," she murmured, and taking Heath's hand once more, she started down the steps.

Creda giggled. "Well? Get on with it."

Heath blanched and yanked his hand away from hers.

Emilia frowned. "Get on with what?"

"You've been trapped," Iris said pityingly. "You've got to kiss squeamish Uncle Heath."

Squeamish Uncle Heath who'd already retreated to the other side of the doorjamb. Emilia's feet went out from under her. She gasped, throwing her arms wide for balance to no avail.

Heath, however, was across the foyer in three quick strides and caught under her knees and back. She glanced at the too-close white marble floor and then up at her unlikely savior.

Her heart hammered. Only, it wasn't from the fall. It was his gaze. The intensity of those blue eyes seared her. *Say something. Say anything…* "I do not recall you being this swift of foot as a boy," she whispered.

"I was."

Their lives had intersected the moment she'd been born, so why didn't she have more memories of him? Nay, of them together. "I did not notice," she confessed, still faintly breathless from her second near fall. Nay, it was the weight of his arms wrapped around her. His body's nearness.

"I know."

With that faintly cryptic response, he set her on her feet. What did that mean? He had been the one who'd ignored her the whole of her existence. Hadn't he? She searched her memory for every last interaction she'd had with Heath, but it was all tangled in her mind.

Her fingers shaking, Emilia smoothed her cloak and then straightened her bonnet.

"We should be going," Heath said in the familiar austere tones she'd come to expect, so at odds with the ones he'd used in the breakfast room… or in the billiards room. Or moments ago, when they'd been hanging mistletoe.

"Yes. We should. Thank you, ladies, for allowing me—"

Creda and Iris slid into Emilia's path, shoulder to shoulder. The young girls would have given the late Bonaparte nightmares.

"The kiss," Creda reminded.

Oh, dear. They'd not forgotten. Why would they? Tales of kisses and any hint of romantic overtures were the manner of stuff to fascinate any girl. As such, they would expect the pair under the mistletoe to make good on that holiday promise. Emilia fanned her cheeks before realizing too late what she'd done. *Stop. You're no simpering miss.*

In the end, it was Heath who answered for both of them. "I do not think that is a wise idea."

An odd pang of disappointment stuck in her chest.

"It is the rule of the mistletoe," Creda said in somber tones.

"It isn't proper, however, for a gentleman to go about kissing a young lady."

As uncle and nieces went back and forth debating the "law of the mistletoe," Emilia frowned. Heath spoke of her as if she were one of those young debutantes a gentleman had to be delicate about. She'd not been that creature in more years than she cared to remember.

You have, however, become obnoxiously proper in the time since Connell threw you over.

As Heath continued to deliver a rather impressive—if insulting—list of all the reasons he should not kiss Emilia, her frown deepened... for altogether different reasons. Why, Heath's lengthy list was really about all the reasons he did not *want* to kiss Emilia.

"And furthermore, we're more like brother and—"

Oh, she'd had quite enough.

Catching him by the lapels of his cloak, Emilia pressed her mouth to his in a kiss that was to have been fleeting and, more important, would silence him and his blasted list. Only, it was neither of those things.

The blood roared in her ears at the absolute heat of his mouth on hers, his firm lips that were—

Good God.

Slightly out of breath, Emilia used the fabric of his cloak to propel him back. *I kissed him.*

More than half dazed, Heath stumbled away from her.

Iris and Creda stared on, wide-eyed. "I didn't know ladies kissed men," Creda whispered.

"Ladies can do anything a man can. I w-would argue even more, given that a woman can birth a babe." How was her voice so steady? Unable to meet Heath's gaze, she focused on the young twins. Managing a nonchalant toss of her curls, she turned to the young girls. "Creda, Iris, I look forward to speaking with you further."

Then, gathering up the ladies skates forgotten until now on the step, she continued out the front door. Setting a brisk clip for herself, she tested whether Heath Whitworth was indeed as quick-footed as he'd professed.

CHAPTER 7

*The happiest unions are those where a gentleman and lady
have shared interests.*
Mrs. Matcher
A Lady's Guide to a Gentleman's Heart

THERE WAS ANY NUMBER OF rules in terms of a gentleman's
relationship with young ladies: sisters of best friends were most
certainly off-limits, as were the widows of late friends.

What Heath, however, had never been able to suitably sort out
were the rules on a best friend's former betrothed.

For everything Heath didn't know about the specifics of that
particular dynamic, there was one singular certainty: A gentleman
did not kiss his best friend's former betrothed. *Ever.*

Particularly this woman. Guilt needled at his conscience. For
Heath, it was an unfamiliar sentiment. After all, he'd always been
endlessly loyal to both friends and family. This, however, his lusting
after Emilia, crossed all manner of lines. What was worse, Heath
wouldn't undo that brief moment if he could.

As such, as Emilia hurried out the door, ice skates in hand, Heath
was more than tempted to allow her to continue on her way, and
take whatever opposite path she took, and forget that moment
under the mistletoe had happened.

Alas, the decision was ultimately made for him by another.

"Here." Iris shoved his ice skates at his chest. Heath grunted, reflexively catching the skates and neatly slicing through the fabric of his glove. "You'll need these."

"The lady is rather impressively swift, and very soon I suspect you shan't catch her." With that, his niece rushed over to join her sister at the long hall table where the previously forgotten strips of garland lay.

"I'll have you know," he called after her as he fumbled with the straps of the skates, "I am quite quick."

"That remains to be seen," Creda muttered as she collected the leather footstool. "For your sake, I hope you are, or you shan't catch her."

Catch her?

Those two words suggested he was in pursuit of the lady in question. Which, in a way, given he'd received a list with his marching orders from the Duchess of Sutton, was not far from the mark.

And yet...

Heath peeked through the glass panels alongside the doorway and caught sight of her rapidly retreating figure.

If he were at least being honest with himself, he'd admit that he was, and rather had been, enjoying these moments with her.

Including their kiss.

Nay, especially that kiss.

He strangled on his swallow.

Good God...

"I should hope you're as impressively swift as you claim," Creda drawled. "Because you're going to need that speed to catch the lady."

I do not recall you being this swift of foot.

He went absolutely still.

Why... why... the minx had issued him a challenge. By God, he'd been so fixed on the memory of her mouth on his and the unexpectedness of that kiss that he'd failed to realize precisely what she'd done: She'd set out to prove she could outpace him.

Skates in hand, Heath sprinted to the door and rushed out.

"Who would have imagined? He is faster than I would—"

He slammed the door shut behind him, drowning out the rest of the backhanded compliment from his disloyal niece.

Squinting, he did a sweep of the snow-covered grounds. The chit couldn't have put too much distance between them. Why, she was hampered by cumbersome skirts.

A memory traipsed in of a long-ago house party her parents had hosted.

"Emilia Abernathy Aberdeen, what in the Lord's creation are you wearing...?"

"Why, pants, Papa. Skirts are far too cumbersome. If you're so adamant I wear them, you should don them yourself and see how bothersome they are."

A smile ghosted his lips and then withered as an altogether different image flitted forward, a forbidden one fabricated by his own roguish inclinations: Emilia, a woman grown, in tight-fitting trousers that hugged her buttocks and hips and those long legs that went on forever.

Stop.

Heath gave his head a firm shake and exhaled slowly. The sough of his breath stirred a small puff of white in the cool air. He wasn't a rogue like the other Whitworth brother. He was nothing if not responsible. Dutiful. In fact, it was those two qualities that saw him dancing attendance upon the impish Lady Emilia.

Therefore, his being out here in the early morn hours, in the freezing winter weather, was simply a product of those obligations.

With that reminder clearing his previously improper—and guilty—musings, he resumed his search.

And then he spied her. She was a fading mark on the horizon. "Goodness, even in skirts, you are still as quick as ever," he muttered into the quiet.

Suddenly, Emilia stopped and turned, the hem of her crimson cloak dancing in the wind.

She shot a hand up and waved at him wildly, startling a laugh from him. Why, she had issued him a challenge. One he was already on his way to losing. "The minx," he whispered without inflection, and then, he bounded down the steps two at a time. The moment his boots touched the graveled drive, Heath took off sprinting.

His boots churned up rock and snow that was ground into the path, and as he raced to catch up with Emilia, the wind caught and carried her laughter on the breeze.

Heath grinned and increased his strides. The cold filled his lungs, invigorating and pure.

When was the last time he'd raced about in the snow? Or...

anywhere, for that matter? Nay, he'd become increasingly fixed on the expectations his family and the world had of him as the ducal heir. This, running carefree through the grounds of Everleigh, was magical. Exhilarating. Joy—

"Oomph." Sputtering around a mouthful of snow, Heath skidded to a stop. His eyes blurred from the remnants of that missile, and he wiped his face. Surely the chit hadn't just—

There was a slight hiss.

Thwack.

His hat went flying from his head.

Recoiling, he glanced around and then down at his hat sitting, top up, on the snow. Why… why, she'd hit him a second time. He didn't know whether to be impressed or affronted at having been caught off guard by her twice now.

"You are out of practice with snowballs, Lord Heath!" Her entirely too amused voice sounded from around the trunk of one of his parents' beloved pines.

Heath dusted remnants from where her missile had exploded snow upon his shoulder. "I'll have you know, ducal heirs do not go about partaking in snowball fights," he informed her as he dropped to a knee to rescue his upended hat.

Emilia stepped out from behind her hiding place and rested a shoulder against the tree. "Don't they?" she drawled, so negligent in her repose and so different than the prim and proper ladies of London.

"Certainty not."

"I trust they are—" She paused. "*You* are," she amended, "seeing to far more important ducal-heir matters."

"Indeed." Attending to that future role had been something that had fallen to him when he'd been just a boy of ten. From the moment his father had taken him under his wing, he'd kept him there, and Heath had lost out on moments such as these that his brother and late brother had known.

So much time had been lost. Graham… His late brother, Lawrence, who'd died too young.

"What are they?"

She sounded so genuine in her curiosity that he briefly stopped his distracted movements. Heath glanced up.

Emilia drifted closer, her crimson cloak whipping about her

ankles. At some point, her bonnet had been knocked back, and a handful of golden curls had fallen about her shoulders. Heath's breath froze in his lungs. She was… Aphrodite. That goddess of love and beauty.

"Surely if they are so great to enumerate, you must recall at least one of them, Lord Heath," she teased.

And yet, with her wit and humor, she had the spirit of Thalia.

Emilia drew to a stop five paces away. When the silence continued, the lady tipped her head at a confused little angle.

God, he was rot at discussion. He always had been and always would be. Particularly with Lady Emilia Aberdeen. "There is the continued study of land holdings."

"Of which yours are vast," she murmured.

"Indeed. There is also—" Jumping to his feet, Heath launched his snowball, catching Emilia square in the chest, shocking a gasp from her.

The young lady glanced from him to the smattering of snow upon her cloak—her now damp cloak—and then to Heath. By the shock rounding her expressive eyes, he might as well have fired a pistol at her breast. "Why… why… Heath Whitworth. Did you… trick me?"

Grinning, Heath dropped a bow. "And I managed to catch you, as well."

She cocked her head.

With his index finger and middle one, he mimicked a rapid walking movement. "Caught you. I raced quickly and—"

"I know what it means to be caught," she said with another toss of those golden curls. A shaft of early morning sunlight caught the edges of those strands and added an ethereal shimmer around her.

His smile froze on his face. She was beauty personified.

Grateful that the cold had already stung his cheeks so that she'd attribute his damned flush to the winter air, Heath scooped up his hat. "I would be remiss if I didn't point out that battling the same person whose favors you seek hardly seems the wisest course to guarantee your skating lesson." He knocked the snow-covered article against his thigh.

"No," she said somberly. "I considered as much." A slow, teasing grin spread across her face. "But then I weighed both pleasures and could not possibly pass up striking you with a snowball."

Heath held two fingers aloft. "Two."

They shared a smile. And a lightness suffused his chest.

It had... never been like this with her. He'd never been like this around her. *I wanted to be, though... I wanted to be the manner of man who could have wooed her.* While she? She had always been her usual charming, witty, and spirited self.

He, however, had been the man who couldn't muster two proper sentences to bring her to even the smallest smile.

"This is nice," she said softly. *It was.* A pensiveness filled her eyes. "I don't remember you being..."

Heath waited for her to finish that musing. When she made no attempt to finish the thought, he, a gentleman who prided himself on his restraint, found himself moving closer to her, needing the remainder of her words. "You don't remember my being...?"

"Like this," she murmured.

Mayhap had I been, she would have noticed me and not another...

His lips froze in a painful smile. As soon as the traitorous thought slid in, Heath quashed it. He was never, nor never would be, the manner of man who could entrance a lady the way Renaud had managed with Emilia. Heath cleared his throat. "Yes, well, there were—"

"Responsibilities?" she murmured, and there was something so faintly pitying in her voice and in her eyes that he had to briefly look away.

How much of his life had he missed in being the dutiful son? He'd forgotten what it was to have simply enjoyed the simplest of pleasures, such as racing through the snow-covered countryside and throwing snowballs. "Responsibilities," he echoed.

So much time lost.

The possibility of her, lost... to another. A man who'd known how to smile and laugh and charm. Or, he once had. Renaud was no longer the man he'd been, either. That only intensified the guilt sitting in his belly.

"Come," Emilia urged. She fetched their skates and handed his over. "You have new responsibilities."

He blanched and, for one agonizingly endless moment, believed she knew that his mother had ordered him to squire Emilia about during the house party.

Emilia gave him a peculiar look. "Teaching me to skate, Heath."

Teaching her to skate?

"Unless you've changed your mind?" she ventured when he didn't immediately reply.

"No! Not at all."

Her smile returned, dimpling her right cheek and glimmering in her eyes. "Shall we, then?" Looping her arm through his, Emilia urged them onward.

As he let her lead him down the path, he felt a kindred connection to Adam, who'd eaten of that forbidden fruit.

CHAPTER 8

*A lady would be wise to welcome the suit of a man
with whom she may match wits.*
Mrs. Matcher
A Lady's Guide to a Gentleman's Heart

EMILIA HADN'T KNOWN HEATH COULD run so quickly.

Or that he could throw a flawless snowball and perfectly hit his target.

She hadn't known simply because in the course of her entire life, she'd never once witnessed the always serious little boy shut away in his school rooms partaking in a single activity that could be considered improper.

Until now.

Seated on the trunk of a fallen oak, Emilia peeked over at Heath, who'd taken up a spot directly opposite her. There could be no doubting his intentions for keeping that space between them.

It was not his usual aloofness toward her, however, that commanded her stare, but rather, the masterful way in which he strapped on his skates. His fingers flew with a dizzying rapidity as he tightened and fastened each of the three leather straps.

Sitting here, staring on unobserved as she admired his effortless skill, Emilia found the whole experience rather... humbling.

She didn't like not knowing how to do something. Those failings felt far greater for what they represented—a woman who'd been far less bold and defiant than she'd credited and who along the way had ceded more control to the expectations Society had of her.

I can do this… I can certainly don and fasten a pair of skates…

After all, how… Heath made it appear so simple.

Heath finished strapping the top latch and looked up.

Their gazes collided.

A crooked half-grin tipped the corners of his lips, so boyish, endearing, and unexpected that Emilia froze, wholly ensnared and unable to look away.

Heath stood, made impossibly taller by the blades he now expertly balanced upon. He joined her at the felled tree. "There is no harm in asking for help, Emilia," he said simply as he dropped to a knee beside her.

"*Not* if you are a ducal heir," she explained as he reached for one of the skates he'd fetched for her. "Where women are concerned, however, the expectation is that one will falter and that one will require help." More specifically, a gentleman's help. Because the whole world, her parents included, believed women to be inferior to their male counterparts. "It is therefore a paradoxical situation where to gain a skill a lady must cede to the world her inability to do something, which only feeds societal assumptions where young ladies are concerned, thereby perpetuating a myth that all women are unskilled in certain sets," Emilia concluded, breathless from her explanation.

Heath paused in the middle of stretching the leather fastenings. "Hmm," he murmured, his head bent once more as he devoted himself to his task.

Hmm? Emilia frowned. Just what precisely did he mean with that noncommittal *hmm?* "What?" she asked reluctantly, and he glanced up.

"*Scientia est potentia.*"

He should speak Latin with a fluent perfection.

"Knowledge is power," she murmured. At the surprise lighting his eyes, she felt her cheeks warm.

"Precisely." Heath tapped the corner of his temple. "Knowledge is power."

"Pretty quotes do not diminish what the world is truly like." Harshly limiting for women and even more so for spinsters who'd been jilted as young, once brightly optimistic debutantes. "The fact remains, women are not allowed to falter, whereas men are forgiven far greater weaknesses and transgressions." She was unable to keep the bitterness from creeping into her voice. Why, they could even break a formal betrothal, and the whole world wondered what the bride-to-be had done to merit that disgrace. "Admitting one's lack of knowledge only further feeds the low opinions the world has."

"But humbling oneself in the search for new information and skills is only temporary. The knowledge is then learned and used and in turn transferred to the world around us, and that shatters any stereotypes you speak of, rather than pride in silence."

Unnerved, Emilia gave silent thanks when Heath returned his attentions to the skate in his hand. Over the years, her sense of pride had shaped how she presented herself to the world. She'd not wanted anyone—not her parents, not her brother, nor her friends, nor Society on the whole—to see the same empty-headed girl prone to committing grand mistakes as she'd done with Renaud. Heath now painted that deliberate decision on her part in a light she'd not before considered. There was an unswerving truth to his quietly spoken words. Words that wound through her, powerful for their accuracy and with a depth she'd not allowed herself to consider.

"I believe this should fit," Heath said as he lifted his head. He reached down and then stopped. He reached again.

When his fingers hovered awkwardly in the air, Emilia bent and searched the ground for the source of his hesitancy. "What is it?"

"Your foot," he blurted.

Her foot...? As she lifted her boot and inspected the reason for his uncertainty, her frown deepened. Granted, being taller than most women and many men, she knew her feet were slightly larger, but she'd never taken Heath Whitworth for one who'd so indelicately point out that detail. "What is wrong with my foot?"

His cheeks went red. "Nothing," he said quickly. "I'm certain it is an entirely lovely foot."

It was a perfectly rote, gentlemanly deliverance.

"Oh?" she drawled. "And just what makes you so certain?"

Heath coughed. "Uh... That is... What I was attempting to say"—good, the miserable bounder should be discomfited—"is...

is… I have to touch you," he said hoarsely.

Of their own volition, Emilia's eyebrows shot up.

He cursed, and her brows crept up another fraction at the impressively colorful invective from his always proper lips. "What I am saying is… That is… I need to handle your foot." As his words rolled together, he gesticulated wildly with her skate. "Or rather, I require your foot"—Emilia angled away to avoid an accident run-in with the blade—"to put your skate on. May I have permission to touch you?"

Emilia grinned widely. "I must confess that is a rather spectacularly surprising request, given you ran the other way when I kissed you."

"I wasn't running away from your kiss," he said, gesturing wildly with the skate again.

"You were not necessarily running toward it, either," she said dryly, enjoying herself more than was appropriate.

The skate slipped from Heath's fingers and went sailing over his shoulder. He recoiled, a response she'd wager her smallest left finger was a product of her words and not having launched her skate a good five paces behind him… into a snowdrift. Heath whipped his head around and then faced her again. "Forgive me," he said gruffly. "May I see your foot for the purpose of putting on your skate?"

There was a faint pleading in his tone and his eyes. Emilia took mercy. "You may." She rested her right foot on his knee. Heath immediately reached behind himself for the respective skate, and searched around with his fingers. There was nothing else for it, Emilia was going to hell for her wicked humor. "It is somewhere behind you," she whispered.

Heath blinked, and she pointed helpfully at the skate.

"That is right." He muttered another curse, and then, in an impressive display of agility, he leaped up and set out after her skate. As he strode through the copse, she admired the way he walked on two blades, managing an ease most men didn't muster walking in bare feet.

Following his retreat with her gaze, Emilia chewed at the tip of her glove and used his distraction to study him.

How very different Heath was from Renaud. In fact, the pairing of the young duke and ducal heir had always befuddled her.

Ever the charmer, her former betrothed had had an artificial-
ness to his words. His tongue had been as smooth as a rapier, and
"mad, bad, and dangerous to know," he'd wielded it with a skill
Byron himself couldn't even manage. As a young woman, she'd
been starry-eyed whenever he'd spoken. As a woman, burned by
his betrayal, she found herself preferring that not every word to fall
from a man's lips was perfectly practiced.

She'd come to find she didn't want pretty compliments and
wicked whispers. She wanted… something more. Something genuine. At the time, she hadn't known as much. At the time, she'd
been a girl blinded by tales of debutantes who tamed scoundrels
and went on to live happily ever afters. But there had never been
anything of any true meaning that they'd shared on any topics.

"Got it," Heath muttered, his deep baritone snapping into her
reverie. Lifting the skate like a trophy collected by a triumphant
conqueror, he raced over with an impressive alacrity for one standing atop metal blades. Heath sank back onto a knee. "May I?" he
murmured.

"Please." With none of her earlier self-annoyance over her inability, Emilia rested the heel of her boot on his knee.

He doffed his gloves and set them alongside her on the trunk.

Did she imagine his hesitation, as if he still could not bring himself to touch her?

Likely not. Furthermore, it was just being around her that he'd
always struggled with. He was here because his mother ordered it.
He'd never come 'round when she was a girl, and then when she
made her debut, and no time after that. "It is just a foot, Heath,"
she said gently.

"It is *your* foot," he said quietly, and then at last, he collected her
heel, handling her boot as if he had a prized treasure in hand to
be guarded.

It is your *foot.* What precisely did he mean by that? It was his
mother's goddaughter's foot? Renaud's former betrothed's foot?

"Now," Heath went on, "the first order of business in donning
skates is to lock the heel in place here. Like so." He guided the
slight heel of her boot into place. Emilia stared at his bent head as
he helped her through those steps. "Then, you need to be sure the
front is perfectly in line and latched. Next comes the fastenings." A
gust of wind stirred the barren trees overhead, and that breeze sent

one of Heath's dark locks falling over his eye.

Emilia should be attending him and his instructions. After all, she'd just lamented her inability to see to the task herself, and yet, God help her, she could focus on nothing more than that lone midnight strand. It added another layer of… realness to this man who, until this particular house party, had been unruffled and infuriatingly meticulous in appearance and how he conducted himself.

"…or else you'll risk fall—" Heath suddenly picked his head up, and the abrupt cessation of his instructions shattered the moment. He frowned. "Were you paying attention?"

She blinked wildly.

Heath Whitworth *would* be the first gentleman to call her out.

"Yes? No." Heat burned her cheeks, and she prayed he'd misconstrue their color as an effect of the cold. "No," she finally settled for, shaking her head. "I may have been distracted." *Was. I was distracted.* Alas, there was one thing good to come from the code by which a gentleman did not press a lady for—

"By what?" he asked, eyeing her like she'd sprung a second head.

By you. I was once again distracted by you, and now this time, the mere texture and color of your hair…

Mayhap that forthrightness she so appreciated was a bit overrated, after all. "My own thoughts," she settled for and was grateful when he didn't press her further.

"What were the last instructions you recall?" Heath asked, once again all business.

"You were just mentioning the leather straps."

"Ah, yes. The first thing to remember about ice skates and wearing them…"

Emilia's breath caught as Heath handled her ankle. There was a contradictory strength and tenderness to his touch that proved wholly distracting.

"…is that your foot, your boot, and your blades all become one. They have to move in concert. After the boot is snug, it is essential to tighten the straps sufficiently." He demonstrated the correct degree of tightness. When he finished, he sank back on his haunches. "Now, your turn, my lady," he said, handing over the other blade.

Emilia accepted the proffered skate. "Do you know that ice skating goes back thousands of years?"

"Indeed?" he asked with such a genuine curiosity underlying his tone that she looked up.

She was so accustomed to her own parents hurrying her tellings along. Her loving brother listened—albeit politely, if not most times patronizingly. Encouraged by the interest in Heath's gaze, she continued, "The purpose of skating was altogether different." She fitted the heel of her boot between the metal clamps. "Oh, they would also make the blades of animal bones, but they would use them to traverse the frozen waters while foraging for food. It wasn't until—"

"The Middle Ages that ice skating became a pastime," he supplied.

"Yes, precisely." She'd become so used to being indulged in her discourse that she'd forgotten what it was to converse with someone who had like interests or studies. "How did you—?"

"I came across it while reading—"

They spoke as one: "*Descriptio Nobilissimi Civitatis Londiniae.*"

"*Descriptio Nobilissimi Civitatis Londiniae.*" She nodded excitedly. "You've read it."

"I've read many things." Heath swiped his gloves from the trunk and beat them together. "I was the bookish brother." He offered that almost apologetically.

"Because you had to be? Or because you wished it?" Emilia didn't know where the question came from. Their being together was predicated on nothing more than his mother's expectations— and the game Emilia even now played at his expense. So why did she want to know that answer from this man who until now had been largely a mystery to her?

"My brothers, they fell into neat little categories. Sheldon...or Graham, as he prefers to be called, was the troublesome scamp who enjoyed anything athletic. And then there was Lawrence..." Such sadness suffused Heath's gaze, she wished she could call back her earlier question.

Lawrence. The brother who'd been tragically killed while riding.

"Lawrence was the scholarly one," he said, his voice as distant as his eyes, and she wanted to erase his sadness and return them to how they'd been speaking about ice skating and mistletoe.

Emilia gathered one of his hands, and despite the cold, despite her glove serving as a barrier between them, the warmth in that slight connection penetrated the fabric. "And what of you, Heath? What manner of boy were you?" *I should know those answers.* He should be more than this mystery he was.

Heath glanced at their interconnected fingers and then lifted his gaze to hers. "I was an odd combination of both," he said wistfully. "The world, however, expects a gentleman to be one and not the other, and invariably, they always prefer the charming rogue to a proper gentleman."

"I don't."

It was harder to say who was more stunned by her admission. What was she saying? What had she said? She didn't want any gentleman—proper, roguish, or otherwise. Did she? Panic knocked away at her chest.

Heath's mouth moved several times before he formed words, before he found them. "But you once did," he pointed out quietly.

Emilia bit the inside of her lip. "The young are often foolish and do not realize…"

"Boring is safer?" he asked with a small smile.

The truth slammed into her. He spoke of himself. He spoke as if his own character was somehow defective. "I discovered, Heath, that a lady's excitement isn't and shouldn't be reserved for the feckless cads of the world." Emilia touched her gaze upon his face, silently acknowledging that she'd been guilty of feeding those opinions. "That one's honor and strength of character are far greater than any fleeting thrill provided by"—her jaw tightened—"some unfeeling rogue."

At some point, they'd begun speaking of Connell. *And I don't want to.* She didn't want to spoil her time with Heath by mention of another. Emilia braced for him to rush to the defense of Renaud.

Heath cleared his throat and then neatly steered them back to their previous discourse. "Despite having something in common with Lawrence and Graham, my responsibilities were first and foremost to the title." He spoke the latter part as if uttering a rote command he'd heard too many times.

Given her own life experience as a duke's daughter who'd had similar such words drilled into her head, she knew Heath no doubt had heard them, too. What must it have been like, and what must it still be, to have the world view one as nothing more than a future title? After all, Emilia had seen her own brother treated too often in that way, and by their own parents.

"It is odd that I've known you my entire life," she said wistfully, "and what you enjoy or what interests you have, I've never known." She'd never seen him race or skate or swim. Or do anything that the other children had done at those summer house parties. What would it have been like—nay, what would they have been like had they taken part in those same pleasures?

He cleared his throat. "Yes, well, younger sons are permitted greater freedoms and, more important, the freedom of choice," he finished.

What had started out as a meeting to teach Heath a lesson had taken on new meaning and, God help her, a new understanding. Despite her years of resenting Heath Whitworth and his coldness, she'd found that they had more in common than she could have ever believed.

Horror rooted slowly in her brain as she acknowledged what would have been otherwise unthinkable until this moment: She genuinely *liked* Heath Whitworth, and God help her, she enjoyed his company.

Unable to meet his eyes, Emilia set to work on her skates.

CHAPTER 9

If a lady is to enter into the state of marriage, she would be
wise to select a gentleman in possession of a sense of humor.
Mrs. Matcher
A Lady's Guide to a Gentleman's Heart

As EMILIA RESUMED LATCHING HER skates, Heath considered his previous discourse with the lady.

He didn't speak of his childhood or his late brother or... well, really, any parts of himself with anyone.

Somewhere along the way, his father and tutors had ingrained those lessons in him, until Heath had become a master at erecting barriers between himself and everyone else. Those rules had even extended to his only living brother, Graham, a brother who'd come to despise him—and rightfully so.

Here in this copse, however, Emilia Aberdeen had managed to compel Heath to speak about parts of himself he'd never shared with another soul.

What was more, she was also the only person who'd ever *asked* about who Heath was as a person.

To everyone else, Heath was a marquess who'd one day be duke. The all-important heir.

He was the ducal heir who always did that which was expected of him. The world neither knew, nor cared, that he'd been snatched from the schoolroom one day by his father, and all those pleasures he'd once found in life had become forbidden. His reputation as the responsible one had only been solidified after Lawrence's death in Heath's bid to ease some of his parents' heartbreak.

It felt so very good now to simply be... a man.

A man like anyone else, and not just a man with a title.

"How do I know if it is tight enough?" she asked, briefly lifting her gaze from her skates.

"If it is uncomfortable, you know you've fastened it enough."

An endearing little frown puckered her brow. "Hmph. If one has to focus on pain, it takes away from some of the pleasure."

Pushing to a stand, Heath jammed his gloves on and then held out a palm. "The more one wears skates, the more comfortable and natural-fitting they become."

"There is nothing natural in either walking or gliding upon a narrow blade just a fraction of the width of one's foot," she muttered under her breath as he drew her to her feet.

"Ah, but where is that earlier enthusiasm?"

"It was replaced by sore feet," she said, and with her palms in his, she allowed him to lead her to the edge of the shore.

As he guided her, Heath grinned. When was the last time he'd enjoyed himself like this? Ever? He stopped five paces away, and Emilia looked questioningly up at him.

"You should try for yourself, so you can have a feel for them." Even as he didn't want to relinquish her hands. Even as there was a natural rightness to the fit of her palms in his.

Horrified, he tried to yank his hands away. Emilia, however, retained an impressive death grip on him. He tried again.

"Why do I get the idea that you're trying to be rid of me, Heath Whitworth?" she asked as she at last relinquished her hold on him.

She knew him not at all if she believed that. She didn't know that she'd been a girl he'd been too in awe of to approach as a boy—and a woman he'd longed for before, and then shamefully, after his best friend had wooed and won her. "Help you," he said, backing toward the frozen lake. "I'm attempting to help you."

"And walking backwards?" She snorted. "Now you're gloating, my lord."

"Hardly." He bristled, giving the lapels of his cloak a tug. "That will come after my jumps on the ice."

Emilia's laugh emerged slightly husky, as if from ill use, but unrestrained and bell-like as it filtered through the copse. Hers was a temptress' smile, and her siren's laugh made a mockery of the honorable existence he sought to live.

The heel of his blade snagged a root and slashed across those shameful musings.

Heath cursed as he came crashing down to the earth, landing hard on his arse for a third time this week.

Emilia's laughter abruptly died. "Heath," she called. With her arms stretched out to balance herself, she ambled toward him on her skates.

He sighed, wanting the earth to open up and swallow him into some hidden realm where humiliation ceased to be a worry.

"Are you all right?" she asked, picking her way over the same damned root that had felled him and stopping above him.

"Quite so." Wounded pride likely healed.

Emilia held a hand out, and his gaze went to the offering she stretched toward him. "Come, now," she said, shaking her fingers when he made no move to take them. "There is no harm in asking for help," she said, waggling her eyebrows. "Or so said a wise man before. Literally just before."

He chuckled, and then slipping his hand into hers, he levered himself upright, careful not to propel the spirited minx back. They made their way to the lake, and Heath held his elbow out. "Shall we?"

Emilia jabbed a finger toward the clouded sky. "*Carpe diem!*" She cleared her throat. "That is, with a bit of help."

Grinning, Heath took her by the hands, and scissoring his legs, he skated backward slowly, pulling Emilia along with him.

A small, breathless laugh filtered from her lips.

Because of him.

Though, in fairness, it was more the whole skating business… But it was with him, and that was enough. He who'd never believed himself charming enough or engaging enough for the spirited Emilia Aberdeen had brought her to laughter.

"You look very pleased with yourself, Lord Heath," she said primly and looked down at the ice. Her right foot slid sideways. Gasping, Emilia retrained her focus on her unsteady feet.

"I am." Immensely. Only never for the reasons she'd dare believe. "It helps if you look up. You're pitching your weight forward," he explained, gliding back and drawing her with him. Heath brought them to a stop alongside a boulder at the opposite shore.

Emilia frowned. "What is this?"

"Part of learning to skate is watching how to move on the blades." With her zeal, she'd always be racing, and as such, the spirited woman would always chafe at being a mere observer of life.

He braced for resistance, but then she perched on the edge of the boulder. "Very well," she said. Loosening the ribbons under her chin, she let her bonnet fall back. The faintest flicker of sunlight penetrated a break in the heavy blanket of clouds overhead, and that lone ray bathed her pale blonde strands in a soft, ethereal glow. "As you were, Lord Heath."

As you were...

All business she was.

It was a necessary and perfectly timed reminder. Not only was the lady uninterested, she was, and would forever be, off-limits. Steeling his resolve with that age-old logic, he returned to her lesson. "It is natural to keep your weight forward or to lean it out," he explained, demonstrating those two erroneous positions. "However, when you're just beginning, the secret of skating is to keep your knees shoulder-width apart." Heath moved his legs into that proper pose. "This is what will really allow you to keep your weight over your skates." He stared expectantly at her.

Emilia shook her head.

"Try the feel of that positioning."

She hesitated a moment and then used the boulder as a crutch to lever herself up. "I'm going to fall, Heath Whitworth."

"Perhaps," he called back. "But our greatest glory is not in never falling, but in rising every time we fall."

"Confucius," she mumbled as she picked her way slowly over to the ice and inched onto the frozen surface of the lake. That was who she'd always been—fearless, unwilling to allow any challenge to stand in front of her. "You are using your scholarly lessons against me."

"I'm using them to help you," he corrected. "The first rule to remember is you do not want your weight too far forward, like this." He leaned over his skates. "Or too far over your heels. Shoulders square. Chest out."

Emilia immediately assumed the correct positioning. "Splendid."

He skated forward. "Now, you're going to push with your right foot, so turn your right skate in, like so." He angled his blade. "Bend your knee slightly."

"Like this?"

"A bit more. When you push, the weight is going to shift over to your left knee. Push yourself forward by the toe of your skate and go."

Emilia gave herself a little shove and pushed slowly forward. A small laugh escaped her. "I've done it," she cried. The sound of her laughter was so infectious, he found himself joining her.

"Brava, madam." He clapped. "Now again, and this time, when you propel yourself, balance on just one skate and allow the glide to continue longer."

They continued on, with Heath guiding her through the lesson, and the morning melted into early afternoon. His fingers were numb, and his cheeks frozen from cold, but God help him, Heath wanted this moment to go on forever.

Riveted, he gazed at Emilia propelling herself across the ice with the ease of one who'd had blades strapped to her feet the whole of her life.

He had no right enjoying this moment with her. He had no right to steal happiness from her, when it had been only a great sacrifice that had ended her betrothal with Renaud.

Heath, however, proved himself more a bastard than he'd ever believed, because he couldn't care. He could not stop seeing her, Emilia, in this moment, her cheeks stung red from the morning cold and a number of golden curls hanging loosely about her shoulders, tossed free through her movements.

She was an Aspasia, one who captivated with her beauty and proved enthralling in her keen wit.

As she sailed past, his gaze went to her mouth, a crimson-kissed rosebud that he wanted to taste and explore and—

This was too much…

His mother's favor asked too much of him. "We should be returning," he said abruptly. "It is… cold."

Continuing to skate by him, Emilia cupped her hands around her mouth. "D-do you *truly* wish to return?" The cold had lent a faint quiver to her voice.

No, he wanted to remain here with her while the rest of the

world melted away and only they two remained. Which was precisely why they had to leave—now.

"We'll be missed," he pressed as she took another pass by him.
"The guests will wonder."

"Oh, come, they'll never expect we're together."

Nay, that much was true. Nonetheless, the more time he spent
with her, the more his control over his desire for this woman frayed.

"You promised me an ice j-jump, Heath."

She was unrelenting. "It is late. It is no longer morn."

That seemed to reach her. Emilia brought herself to a stop and
glanced around at the heavily wooded grounds. "Then"—she
pointed toward the sky—"*carpe noctem!*"

A hopeless laugh shook his frame as he swiped a hand over his
face. "It is hardly night."

"Well, the longer you stay out here, failing to make good on
your promise, the closer we get to it."

Pushing himself forward, Heath scissored his legs with an increasing rapidity, building momentum, and then he launched himself
into the air.

The exhilarating rush of cold air filling his lungs and slapping his
face reminded him all over again of how much he loved skating in
the dead of winter.

The moment his blades touched the ice, Emilia erupted into
applause. Her laughter filtered around the copse. "Now, that is
skating."

Damned if her praise didn't send pride rushing through him.
He grinned as the peal of her laughter pulled another round of
merriment from his chest.

Stay with her out here. That is what you want.

He warred with himself, and honor, as it always did, invariably
won out. "Come," he said gruffly. Skating back, he held his elbow
out.

"Oh, fine." She stuck her tongue out. "You are ever the addle-
plot, Heath Whitworth. *Amet viros neque sanctiores.*"

He winced. "Destroyer of fun?" No truer words had ever been
spoken, and they were very apropos ones from the woman who'd
failed to see him in all the years she'd been alive.

"I always thought even an insult when spoken in Latin has a
lovely sound to it."

Yes, she was correct on that score.

"Do you make it a habit of speaking in Latin?" he asked, seeking out that detail he would have liked to have known about the lady over the years if fate hadn't marked her forbidden.

"Oh, quite regularly." They neared the boulder, and as they did, Emilia disentangled her arm and skated off. "It quite drives my mother mad."

"I can only imagine." Knowing the duchess as he did, Heath could hear the shrill scolding such Latin phrases were met with. "Undoubtedly, she regrets whichever clever governess is responsible for that elucidation."

Emilia stilled, the bonnet dangling from her fingers. "It wasn't any governess," she said softly. That would be the likely—if erroneous—conclusion to come to. The Duchess of Gayle would have never tolerated a governess who instructed her daughter in anything other than topics deemed suitable for a proper English lady. "I taught myself," she murmured, fiddling with the velvet ribbons.

"You taught yourself?" he echoed.

An air of sadness hovered between them, and before she even uttered her next words, Heath knew the source of that sorrow.

He balled his hands, wishing he'd not teased or asked about her skill with Latin.

"It was after Connell," she said quietly.

Renaud. The ghost between them. Only, Renaud was no ghost. *He is very much alive and very much real… and very much still in love with the woman before you.* "Oh," he said dumbly. For, really, what was there to say?

Emilia jammed her bonnet atop her head. "Forgive me. It's hardly appropriate to speak about… it… him… that… *any of it*… us… with you."

Us. A word that bespoke of Emilia Aberdeen and another, the one who'd won her heart and then had broken it.

You know that betrayal was not without purpose. You know Renaud was as gutted as the woman before you.

As fluid as one who'd skated the whole of her life, Emilia pushed herself forward with the tip of her skate and glided past him.

Heath stared after her retreating frame. She'd given him an out. She'd offered a window into her pain and then allowed him the option to close it.

Selfishly, he didn't want to hear another word about how the affable duke's *defection* had prompted her skill with Latin. And yet, when her gaze had caught and held his, Heath had seen something there. A sad little glimmer in those cornflower-blue depths that should only sparkle with merriment. She wanted to speak... about Renaud.

Heath briefly closed his eyes.

Damn my pathetic, pitiably weak soul.

"Surely you don't intend to casually drop the reason for your mastery of Latin and just skate off without another word," he called after her.

Emilia came to a slow, jerky halt.

He remained where he stood, allowing her to make whatever move she wished, more than half hoping she would choose silence.

With the tip of her skate, Emilia guided herself back around so that they faced each other. "Every gossip paper wrote of it," she said, her tones carrying over, and yet, for what she spoke of, they were surprisingly steady, and almost matter-of-fact. Which was impossible. She had always loved, and no doubt still loved, Renaud to distraction. "Day in and day out. Everyone was speaking of it. My parents, my friends, the whole world, it seemed." She rubbed her gloved palms together as if she sought to bring warmth to her digits. "I didn't want to hear their words and think about..." She went silent for a moment.

Unbidden, Heath forced his feet to move, and he drifted over to her. "Yes?" he urged her quietly as he stopped, his blades kicking up shavings of ice.

Emilia lifted her chin mutinously. Had there ever been a woman prouder? "I wanted a new language that no one around me was speaking or reading or writing." A breeze dislodged her bonnet.

"And so you taught yourself Latin."

She nodded, a proud little smile on her lips. "And so I taught myself Latin," she echoed.

He could very well let her telling end there. He very well *should* let her telling end there. "Why Latin?"

"Well," she went on, her tones lighter than they'd been before, "it is, of course, essential that any proper lady know French." She gave a roll of her eyes, and he found himself grinning at that tell-tale disgust. "Italian and German are encouraged"—she held a finger up—"but *only* for the sake of singing and understanding performances conducted in those tongues, and even then only sometimes German. Alas, there were two languages…" She added another finger, holding two aloft. That movement cost Emilia her balance. Her left skate went out from under her, and Heath caught her by the waist, keeping her upright. His fingers curled reflexively.

Emilia's breath caught. Or was that his own?

Release her. Think of Renaud.

His heart hammered in his ears. Heath could think only of her. He drew her closer, so close their bodies were pressed to each other, and he saw, felt, and heard each intake of her rapidly drawn breath. "And what of the other two languages?" he whispered against her ear.

"Greek," she exhaled. "The other Latin. They were deemed"— her gaze drifted over his face—"wholly unsuitable and nothing any proper lady should"—her lashes fluttered—"or could master." Emilia tipped her face up.

I am lost.

Heath covered her mouth with his, claiming that luscious rose-bud flesh he'd both dreamed of and lamented for almost fifteen years.

A little moan spilled from her lips, a heady symphony of her desire… for him, and it only fueled an insatiable hunger.

Keeping one hand about her waist to keep Emilia upright, he cupped his other under the generous swell of her buttocks and guided her into the vee of his legs.

"I should stop this," Heath rasped against her mouth.

"I'll not forgive you if you do, Heathcliff Whitworth." With that, Emilia tangled her fingers in his hair, and gripping his head, she opened her mouth.

He slipped his tongue inside, and they tangled in a primitive ritual. Sparring. Branding each other. Just as he'd longed to. Only, this embrace contained a bliss far greater than any wicked dream he'd carried of this moment.

"Heath." She moaned his name, both a plea and a demand for more.

Angling his head, Heath deepened the kiss.

He was on fire.

He was—

His legs went out from under him, shattering their contact.

He went down hard on his arse, an increasingly all-too-familiar state with and around this woman.

Heath grunted as the punishing ice sent pain radiating along his legs. Emilia came tumbling down atop him.

They lay there in a tangle of limbs, Emilia draped over his frame. Neither spoke, and when their rasping breaths at last settled into even cadences, Heath helped Emilia up and then followed behind her. This time as they made for the shore, neither of them spoke.

A short while later, they began the long trek back to Everleigh. In silence.

CHAPTER 10

*If one is resolved to make a match, honorable gentlemen
make the best husbands.*
Mrs. Matcher
A Lady's Guide to a Gentleman's Heart

EMILIA WAS NO LONGER THE naïve girl who'd once believed
in gypsy legends and indulged herself in frivolous matters.

Nay, she was nearly thirty and responsible for one of the most
heavily read columns in the *London Post*. As such, she'd already
indulged in more than enough frivolities by tormenting Heath.
That was the sole reason why, after her return from ice skating
with him, she'd sought out her rooms and had remained there
ever since.

Groaning, she dropped her head atop her completed article and
knocked her forehead in a light, rhythmic tapping. "Liar. Liar. Liar,"
she groaned into the brown leather journal.

For now that she'd completed another post, there was no reason
that she need remain in her rooms, except for the most obvious
and humiliating one: she was hiding.

Oh, not because she was a prudish miss who'd been horrified by
any *impropriety*. After all, there had been many kisses before Heath.
Jonah, her father's stable boy, had stolen a kiss when she was a girl
of thirteen. And then there had been Connell. Connell, with his
rogue's reputation, who'd only ever been polite until she'd pressed

her lips to his. From there, he'd kissed her whenever there was a moment they two could steal.

Each one of those kisses, however, had been restrained, as if she were some fragile treasure to be cherished.

But Heath's kiss…

Her breath quickened. Proper, always respectable to a fault Heath Whitworth had made her toes curl. In him, there'd not been a single reservation. Rather, he'd been a man undone by passion, unapologetic in his hungering, and emboldened by her like desire.

She, Emilia Aberdeen, had wanted that embrace to stretch on. And just like that, she'd gone from the secret puppet master tugging on his strings and maneuvering him into completing each action on Lady Sutton's list to the puppet.

She'd sought out her rooms, changed into warmer, drier garments, and hadn't left since for the simple reason that she couldn't face him. Didn't want to face him, because she needed to sort out precisely what had happened. Or what was happening. It was all so jumbled in her mind that she couldn't make sense of any of it.

For, what had begun as a game had morphed into something altogether *different*. Somewhere along the way, she, who'd been annoyed with the always aloof marquess, had found herself not only enjoying their time together, but also yearning for more of it.

And that had been before his kiss…

She slowly lifted her head and touched a fingertip to her lips. "Magic," she whispered. The manner of embrace that curled a lady's toes tight with pleasure. The kind of kiss she'd wished Connell's had been, but never was. One that had sent butterflies dancing in her belly. She groaned. "Fool. Fool. Fool," she mumbled, banging her head once more against her book.

It was just a kiss. Nothing more. Just two sets of lips pressed together as one. Which hardly merited a reason to be hiding.

Emilia registered too late the slightly mincing but measured footsteps belonging to only one duchess outside her room.

Just like that, remembrances of magical kisses faded.

"*What* is the meaning of this?" her mother demanded as she entered the rooms without so much as the benefit of a knock.

"I'm not coming, Mother," she said calmly, not picking her head up from her book.

"Not coming, she says." The duchess belatedly closed the door behind her.

Oh, it was a dire day indeed when the duchess' chastisement outweighed her concern over appearances and her own image.

"You most certainly are joining the festivities, Emilia Abernathy Aberdeen. I did not say anything when you opted to skip the first three nights of parlor games."

"Actually, you did. You demanded I attend." And Emilia had either said no or simply failed to join in.

"And when every other guest is breaking their fast at a decent time?" Her mother swept over, and Emilia leaned over her journal to obscure the words there. "*You* are nowhere to be seen."

"Because I've already taken my morning meal by that point, Mother," she said impatiently, making a final note in her journal lest she forget for later. After all, it was nigh impossible to craft any meaningful guidance on matters of the heart with one's haranguing mama underfoot.

When her mother spoke, there was a faint pleading to her voice. "It is unnatural to dine alone."

I was not alone. Every other day she was, but not this one. Today, there had been Heath and laughter and teasing and more fun than she'd enjoyed in too many years. Emilia swung her legs around and faced her mother. "There is nothing natural about my circumstances, Mama," she said softly.

"Because you do not allow yourself to be normal," her mother cried and then buried the echo of those words with her fingers.

Emilia stiffened. "I am… normal… enough."

"No, Emilia," her mother said flatly. "No, you are not. And 'normal enough' are just two words substituted for 'abnormal.'"

She gave a toss of her curls. "Well, I do not want to be ordinary." She wanted to be an independent woman, without any need—emotional or otherwise—of a man. Didn't she? She had for so long. Or she'd believed she had. Today, skating with Heath and speaking of her past and the hurt she carried, had filled her with a warmth that lingered even now. Unnerved, she reached for her book. "If you'll excuse me, Mother? I am—"

"Busy," her mother cut in. "I know." Color spilled onto her cheeks. "You. Are. Wearing. Your. Words."

She was…?

Puzzling her brow, Emilia lifted her gaze to the nearby cheval mirror. Oh, blast. Coming out of her seat, Emilia strode over to that gilded frame and proceeded to angrily wipe the ink from her forehead.

"My daughter is not antisocial, Emilia Aberdeen," her mother snapped, as if speaking in those clipped duchess tones might somehow make them true.

The Emilia of old had not been. The young woman who'd been jilted by Renaud was an altogether different matter. "I've no interest in joining in holiday games and festivities, Mother," she muttered, licking her finger and making another go at removing the ink.

"No, you do not. You want to be the angry spinster who shuts herself away from the world and pens her words in that book so she doesn't have to face the real world. All the while, you are the one responsible for keeping the memory of Renaud's jilting alive."

A denial sprang to her lips... and then stayed there, unspoken, existing only in her mind. For, as much as she wanted to snap and snarl about the *ton's* sick fascination with her past, the truth remained that she had let that one moment of her life... define her. Emilia pressed her fingertips against her temples.

"You know nothing about it," she said and turned dismissively. What was worse, her mother had never attempted to change that.

With a noisy rustle of satin, her mother rushed forward, planting herself in front of Emilia. "You think I don't know that my daughter's heart was broken?" she asked. Her voice contained a hurt Emilia had never before heard from the all-powerful duchess.

I never truly loved him. Emilia knew that now. She'd loved the idea of being in love. She'd loved Renaud's ability to charm and had been thrilled by him, the wicked rogue her parents and all the world had wisely warned her away from.

"You think your father and I didn't know you loved that bounder beyond reason?" her mother demanded when she still didn't speak.

Emilia glanced down at her slippers. "I didn't know you cared either way," she said softly.

Her mother jerked like she'd been backhanded across the cheek. "Of course I cared. And someday, if you have a daughter, you'll wonder that you ever dared utter those words to me." With that, the duchess started for the door, stopping when she had her fingers on the handle.

As she turned back, Emilia braced for that familiar appeal.

"Come or do not come, Emilia," her mother said resignedly. "Despite your ill opinion of me, I do not want you to attend those events for me. I don't even want you to find a husband for me." A half sob, half laugh spilled from the duchess' lips. "My goodness, if I was so determined to see you in a match I desired, do you truly believe I would have set my sights on Lady Sutton's roguish son for you and not her *boring, perfectly proper one?*"

Any other moment in her life, she'd have fixed on the sudden and staggering realization that her mother cared more than she'd ever credited.

Only...

Emilia's lips slipped at the corners. Was that truly how the world saw Heath? "Lord Heath is not *boring*." And he certainly wasn't *perfectly proper*. A man who'd snuck off with her, sans chaperone, and given her an early morning skating lesson... *And then kissed you like you were the only woman in the world.*

Her mother snorted. "I'm his godmother. I know precisely what he is," she announced with a note of finality. "He's the dutiful boy now entertaining the other ladies present, as his mother would wish." The throwaway statement was meant to highlight the very point Emilia had debated her on.

And yet, Emilia went still. Every muscle turned to stone. He was dancing attendance with the other ladies. It was hardly surprising, given the handful of ladies and the even more spare number of bachelors.

It doesn't matter with whom Heath keeps company.

The burning envy coursing through her set that lie ablaze.

"Either way, you have my word that all my attempts at match-making between you and Lord Heath are at an end. I'll not see you any more unhappy." *Than you already are.*

Those words hung in the air as clear as if the duchess had spoken them aloud.

"Thank you, Mother," she said softly.

The duchess waved a gloved palm. "Do not thank me for doing what any mother ought."

With that, her mother took her leave.

Emilia stood there, fixed to her spot, replaying that exchange in her mind...

She'd been… freed.

After nearly ten years, the none-too-subtle efforts to see Emilia matched and married to whomever the Duke and Duchess of Gayle felt in a given moment would be a suitable husband were at an end.

As such, there should be joy.

Smile. You should be smiling.

Emilia glanced to the gilded mirror and silently told her brain to tell her lips to form the deserved smile.

Only, the muscles ached, along with an odd pressure in her chest. A pressure that had absolutely nothing to do with the idea of Heath turning his effortless charm upon the pair of diamonds of the first water who'd been seeking his attention just days earlier.

An ugly, taunting image slipped forward of Heath guiding another lady through a skating lesson and then taking her into his arms—

Growling, Emilia grabbed her gloves and jammed her fingers angrily into each respective hole.

Mayhap her mother had been correct. Mayhap Emilia partaking in the holiday singing with the other guests was not an altogether bad idea, after all. Quickening her steps, Emilia made her way through the empty corridors.

A mournful wailing met her ears, briefly freezing her in mid-stride. Emilia slowed and searched about for the forlorn creature responsible for the sounds of sadness. She resumed walking, and with each step that brought her closer to the music, the strident shrieks grew increasingly louder.

Singing. Someone was singing.

Reaching the entranceway, Emilia stopped at the threshold.

Her heart tugged.

Miss Francesca Cornworthy, fellow spinster, was the oft-teased young woman that had been the unfortunate one tapped to perform at that given moment. Seated at the pianoforte, the bespectacled lady had her face nearly pressed against the sheet music as she squinted.

She could commiserate with the poor dear as she mustered painfully through what might or might not have been a rendition of "Hymn for Christmas Day."

HARK! the Herald Angels sing

Glory to the new-born King!
Peace on Earth, and Mercy miii—

As the young woman's words rolled together, nearly indecipherable, giggles went up at the front of the room, where Ladies Ava and Lauren had secured front-row seating for the night's performance.

Joyful all ye Nations rise,
Join the Triumphs of the Skies;
Nature rise and worship him,
Who is born at...

Stopping in midchord to turn the page, Miss Cornworthy wrestled with the page for an endless moment.

A hum went up about the room. As Emilia glanced about at the pitying expressions, and several mocking ones, her stomach muscles clenched in misery for the younger woman.

She could not let this go on.

Emilia took a step forward, but her plans to join the girl were halted by a deep baritone that added itself to the silence, finishing the unsung lyric.

"Bethlehem."

All the guests swiveled in their seats to find the owner of the voice.

Her breath caught. *"Heath?"* she whispered, his name on her lips lost to song.

Christ by highest Heav'n ador'd,
Christ the everlasting Lord;
Late in Time behold-him come,
Offspring of the Virgin's Womb.

His rich, resonant tones soared, compelling Emilia to stop at the back aisle. Unable to move, she simply stared on as he quit his seat in the middle of the room and joined Miss Cornworthy at the front.

The young woman looked at him with all the deserved awe and wonderment owed a conquering hero. When he approached her, Miss Cornworthy said something to Heath, but the words were lost in the length of the room and his song.

A moment later, Miss Cornworthy was relinquishing her spot on the bench to Heath. The pair proceeded to sing. The young woman's shrieky soprano blended with Heath's smooth baritone.

And he played pianoforte. Emilia fisted her skirts. Was there nothing he could not do?

Veil'd in Flesh the Godhead see,
Hail th' incarnate Deity!
Pleas'd as Man with Men t'appear,
Jesus our Emmanuel here.

Standing there, with Heath singing and playing the pianoforte, something shifted in her chest. A warmth stirred in a heart that had been cold for so long she'd accepted it would never again feel.

Only to be proven wrong. Only to find Heath Whitworth was nothing like the person she'd made him to be in her mind. And—

A hand snaked around her wrist, startling a gasp from her.

"Generally, one sits through these infernal performances," her brother whispered from the corner of his mouth, and Emilia became aware of three humiliating truths: She remained standing in the middle of the aisle. Several guests were stealing annoyed looks at her.

And Heath was gazing over the top of the pianoforte. *At me. He is staring at me.*

Her belly fluttered wildly under that scrutiny.

He winked.

Worse, he'd caught her staring right back at him. The slightly knowing, teasing flicker of his lashes compelled her at last into her seat.

Her cheeks aflame, Emilia buried her chin in her chest in a bid to make herself as small as possible.

"Making yourself invisible is a wise idea," her brother whispered, leaning down. "But I believe with this performance unfolding, even scandalous you are spared from the *ton*'s attention," he drawled, thankfully mistaking the reason for her embarrassment.

"Oh, hush." Emilia shoved her elbow into his side.

"Ouch."

Only, as quick as Heath's attention had been bestowed upon her, it was gone. All his focus was now directed toward the sheets of music and his performance with Miss Cornworthy.

Where the guests had previously been distracted or whispering about the young woman's singing, now the room sat in rapt silence, hanging on every melodious lyric that spilled forth from Heath's lips.

Hail the Heav'n-born Prince of Peace
Hail the Sun of Righteousness!
Light and Life around he brings,
Ris'n with Healing in his Wings.

Of its own volition, her head came up, and Emilia shifted to the edge of her seat.

Heath was nothing short of magnificent. There was a smoothness to his voice that drew a person into his song and muted all the background noise of the rest of the world. With his confidence and ease at her side, even the painfully shy Miss Cornworthy settled into her song.

"One would expect such from Mulgrave."

Her brother's droll tones cut across Emilia's musings. She turned a frown on her brother. "What is that supposed to mean?"

Barry shrugged. "That the staid Lord Mulgrave would enjoy singing."

Her scowl deepened. Wasn't that the way of the world? Preferring the scoundrels who could toss back a glass of spirits without a wince and mocking a gentleman who had a mastery of the pianoforte and song.

The world, however, expects a gentleman to be one, and not the other, and invariably, they always prefer the charming rogue to a proper gentleman.

"And you think there is something wrong with a gentleman who sings?"

Her brother, whose attention had drifted back to the performance, glanced back in confusion. "What?"

She pursed her mouth. He'd just thrown those censorious words about Heath away and forgotten them.

Their mother leaned over to fix an all-too-familiar glare on them. "Shh." She didn't bother to wait to see that her children complied. And why should she? That glower was dark enough to scare Satan out of sinning. Any other time, that was.

"What would be acceptable behavior of Lord Heath? Would you find the gentleman more acceptable if he drank and played cards?"

"Drank and played cards?" her rogue of a brother mouthed, then said, "You do know I'm speaking about Heath Whitworth, the Marquess of Mulgrave."

"I do?" she snapped. "And what of it?"

Several guests glanced over to where Emilia and Barry quarreled.

Their mother leaned over and pinched her only son, and cherished heir, on the leg. "Will you two hush right now?"

"Gladly," Barry mumbled, folding his arms at his chest and training all his attentions on the impromptu duet.

Come, Desire of Nations, come,
Fix in us thy heav'nly Home;
Rise the Woman's conqu'ring Seed,
Bruise in us the Serpent's Head.

Emilia pinched her younger brother on his opposite leg.

"Bloody hell. What was *that* for?"

"Because I asked you a question, and you didn't answer it."

Barry discreetly waved his hand toward the subject of their discussion. "It's Mulgrave," he said impatiently from the corner of his mouth. "The last to join in anything remotely fun. You said so yourself."

"But that was—" *Before.* Before she'd truly known him or skated with him.

Her brother looked at her peculiarly.

"That was before, when I was just a girl," she finished.

Barry's eyebrows came together. "And you know him so well now, do you?" he asked, eyeing her like a brother eyed a sister whose honor he sought to defend.

Oh, bloody hell. Her brother should choose *this* moment of all moments to be astute and overprotective. She sent a prayer skyward for the dim lighting of Lady Sutton's chandeliers that hid her red cheeks.

Adam's Likeness now efface,
Stamp thy Image in its Place;

"What I do know, Barry," she began in impressively even tones, "is that at this precise moment, when you and the rest of the gentlemen present were content to keep to your seats while dear Miss Cornworthy suffered through the crowd's unkindness, it was *Lord Heath* who came to her rescue. So mayhap I've had incorrect opinions of both of you."

Second Adam from above,
Work it in us by thy Love.

Heath and Miss Cornworthy finished, saving Emilia from answering any further questions from her brother about Heath.

Her gaze forward, she joined the rest of the guests in clapping for that duet.

Heath stepped back, briefly motioned to the bespectacled woman with rose-colored cheeks, and added to the applause.

He'd saved the young woman from more embarrassment. He'd lent his voice and support when everyone else had simply sat there in either abject pity or callous amusement.

A piece of her heart fell into Heath's hands.

Emilia abruptly ceased her clapping and gripped the curved back of the gilded chair in front of her.

Nay, it was impossible.

She didn't have a heart capable of loving any man. Emilia was far too clever and jaded by betrayal to ever allow herself to feel anything for any man. This warmth, however, was all too real and reserved solely for Heath Whitworth.

Over the tops of the heads of the duchess' guests, Heath's gaze wandered out and settled squarely on Emilia.

"Oh, God."

She started at having accidentally spoken aloud. Mayhap no one would no—

"I feel the same way," Barry mumbled, shifting in his chair. "I feared they'd never finish."

Emilia frowned as she concentrated on far safer thoughts than her *feelings* for Heath. His performance had been enthralling, magical, and her brother would find fault.

The duchess glided to the front of the music hall. "Who else shall grace us with a holiday song?" she invited, and Miss Cornworthy took that as her cue to flee back to her spot in the very last row, nearest the exit.

Clever lady.

"Mayhap Mulgrave will give us another song," Barry drawled.

Oh, she'd really had quite enough.

Emilia shot a hand up, and all eyes went to her. "My brother was so moved by the previous performance that he spoke throughout about being compelled to song himself," she called to the duchess.

"How can anyone in the room argue with that?" Emilia's mother clapped her hands, urging her son forward.

When Barry remained rooted to his spot, Emilia nudged him with her knee. "Get on with it. Your audience awaits."

If looks could burn, Emilia would have been a charred pile of ash at her younger brother's feet.

All the while, their mother beamed. "Oh, splendid, Barry! You always were a masterful singer. Not necessarily as skilled as Lord Heath, but skilled enough."

Emilia's lips twitched at the backhanded compliment.

"I am going to kill you," he gritted out.

"Oh, come now. No, you won't. You will, however, sing." With that, she gave his arm a little shove and urged him onward.

With Lady Sutton's guests politely clapping their encouragement, Barry made his way down the aisle with all the reluctance of a man being marched to the gallows, passing Heath on the way.

Her brother paused to glower at Heath before taking up a position in the spot vacated by Miss Cornworthy.

Emilia grinned. Good, it served the lummox right for having been so dismissive and judgmental of Heath. *You were no different...*

Her smile froze in place. Why... why... she *hadn't* been. She followed his approach down the aisle, considering him and all the time she'd known him. She'd taken Heath as a person content to be the ducal heir on the periphery, taking in life around him, but never taking part. Only to have discovered in talking with Heath that he—like her—longed for more.

Emilia's heart fluttered as he stopped at the end of her row.

"May I have this seat?"

"Yes," she blurted, and she climbed to her feet, allowing him to steal Barry's vacant chair.

Of all the guests present, Heath had chosen to sit next to her, even abandoning his earlier seat at the center of the music room.

Unaccompanied, Barry broke out into a rousing, speedy rendition of what was otherwise a solemn carol.

Joy to the World; The Lord is come;
Let Earth receive her King.

Emilia's shoulders shook with amusement.

"What is he doing?" her mother whispered furiously to her husband, who'd previously been slumbering in his seat.

"Wh—I don't know," the duke sputtered.

Let every Heart prepare him Room,
And Heaven and Nature sing.

"He is making a mockery of the song. It may as well be a tavern performance."

With her mother rambling on in annoyance, Emilia directed her gaze forward and tried to think of anything other than the man who occupied the seat beside her. Or the feel of his knee pressed against hers in an unintentional touching of their bodies. For she didn't want to ever again want another man.

It is too late...

Emilia pressed her eyes shut.

Oh, God.

"Is there a reason your brother is glaring daggers at me?" Heath's breath fanned the sensitive shell of her ear, sending delicious little shivers radiating down her neck.

She forced her eyes open.

"It might have something to do with his finding amusement in your joining Miss Cornworthy," she said in a hushed voice. Emilia forced herself to look up at him.

A smile dimpled Heath's cheek in that endearing boylike charm that continued to do maddening things to her heart. "You defended me."

"I... may have," she said grudgingly.

Joy to the Earth, The Saviour reigns;

Let Men their Songs employ.

"He has already sung that lyric, Lord Gayle," Emilia's mother was whispering to her dozing husband. "Why is he singing the same words over and over?"

Heath shifted his body closer. "Why?" he murmured.

The rest of the room was forgotten to Emilia as she held his gaze.

"Because you did what no other man did this night. You..." A buzzing filled her ears, the hum muffled by her brother's slightly discordant singing, as the truth dawned.

He'd rescued Francesca Cornworthy. Because that was the manner of gentleman he was. Whether he wished it or not, he allowed himself to be the honorable figure who'd swoop in and save the lady in need of saving.

Like me...

Her stomach churned.

For Emilia was no different than Francesca Cornworthy. Whatever feelings had sprung within her for Heath were for a man who didn't truly wish to be with her. This was different. It left an empty hole in her chest... because she wanted to be more to him. She didn't want to be an obligation. *I want him to want to be with me as much as I want to be with him.*

A question lit his gaze. "What is it?" Heath asked with a tenderness that nearly brought tears to her eyes.

Damn Heath Whitworth and his insufferable niceness. Jerking her gaze from his blasted beloved face, she blinked those drops back.

What was more, Emilia did not cry. And certainly not over a man.

She embraced the outrage that took root, safe and welcome. "I wanted to know if you would accompany me."

"When?"

That was it. Not *where?* Not *perhaps.* Just, *when?*

Dutiful lord. Ever dutiful.

"On the terrace. Meet me after the next three sets." Good, let the dunderhead suffer through another three performances.

As his mouth formed an unasked question, Emilia rose and slipped from the music hall.

CHAPTER 11

*What a dull marriage it would be to wed a man whose
only interests are drinking and wagering. I advise each
lady to find a gentleman in possession of many talents
and no vices.*
Mrs. Matcher
A Lady's Guide to a Gentleman's Heart

THREE CAROLS.

Heath had sat for three additional songs, performed by his
mother, father, and younger brother, no less.

Through it, he'd been forced to sit alongside Emilia's brother,
who'd scowled at him all the while.

As such, the moment Graham had concluded acting out the
lyrics of "I Saw Three Ships," sung by his three lively stepchildren,
Heath had slipped away from the festivities, unsure who was more
eager for his departure—he or Emilia's brother, Barry.

Nor did Heath's desire to quit the music room have anything to
do with the performances, but rather, his desire to see her.

After dashing above stairs to gather his cloak and gloves, Heath
sprinted through the corridors. He raced toward a pair of young
maids, and they went wide-eyed as he approached.

He slowed his stride enough to touch his brow in greeting
before continuing on.

He'd never done something as inappropriate as to dash about

the ducal halls. And how bloody wonderful this felt, how freeing.

Emilia Aberdeen, the spitfire who'd snagged his hopeless heart as a young lad, had all these years later taught him what it was to live without a care for his responsibilities and to celebrate the pleasures he'd once allowed himself.

What would Renaud say about all that? Any of it? a voice taunted at the back of his mind.

Heath, however, proved more of a selfish bastard than he'd ever believed himself to be, for he continued forward, not stopping until he reached the doors leading to the terrace.

Grinning, he pushed the doors open. "I—" His words abruptly ended. A pair of servants, a plump maid bundled in her cloak and one of the strapping footmen, stared back guiltily. "Oh. Er…" As the couple dropped a respective bow and curtsy, Heath glanced about, searching for the one person he'd sought. *The one person you have no business seeking out…*

"Lord Heath," Emilia called from the opposite end of the thirty-foot terrace.

His heart lifted the way it always did when she was near. "Lady Emilia," he murmured, walking to meet her.

"Are you ready?"

Heath looked around, taking in the details that had first escaped him—the saw resting alongside the balustrade. The neat curl of rope. A shovel.

"What is all this about?" he blurted. For whatever it was the minx intended, it included the pair of servants. He should be grateful that his growing temptation for this woman would be checked firmly by the company of servants. He should be. But he was decidedly not.

"We are going tree hunting."

As mired as he was in his own regrets, it took a moment for Emilia's revelation to sink in. His ears must have heard wrong. "What?"

He knew he sounded like a damned lackwit incapable of anything more than the sporadic *what?*, but really, he'd not a deuced clue what she was up to.

Emilia slipped her arm through his. "We are going tree hunting for your m-mother," she explained, her teeth chattering in the cold.

He allowed himself to be propelled along for several steps, while the servants behind them gathered up the supplies littered about the patio, before grinding his feet to a halt. "I'm sorry. We are going where?"

Emilia sighed. "We are going to find an evergreen to bring back to your family's residence for the Christmastide season."

She spoke as if he should know that. As if she were speaking about some peculiar tradition his family took part in... which they decidedly did not.

"Your sister-in-law, Martha?"

Heath glanced around for the latest edition to their quartet.

"She is not joining us, Heath," she said with an exaggerated sigh. "It is her family's tradition."

"What family? We're her family."

Emilia pounced. "*Precisely*, and as such, each Whitworth should care enough to learn about what is important to her family's traditions."

He puzzled his brows. "What in blazes manner of custom is that?"

"It is a medieval Livonian one," she said in beleaguered tones, as if she expected him to know about ancient Livonian customs. But then again, mayhap clever as she was, the self-taught scholar was in possession of even the most obscure details. "It became quite popular with the Lutheran Germans."

Lutheran? His frame shook with amusement. "Lutheran customs?"

She wrinkled her nose. "Do you have a problem with Lutherans?"

"I have no problems with anyone. My proper father, however, would have never relented to allowing—"

"Your father was quite enthused by the idea of a tree when I broached it with him earlier in the week."

That immediately quelled his mirth. She'd not only spoken to his father, but she'd secured his approval for an unconventional custom. Whatever piece of him hadn't already been hopelessly in love with Emilia Aberdeen was lost in this moment. Was there nothing she couldn't manage, no dragon she couldn't tame?

Alas, that devotion proved—as always—vastly one-sided.

"Your sister-in-law shared with me how each holiday she and

her children would go out hunting for a tree to bring home and decorate, and I believed this would be a lovely way to make her feel more at home here."

Heath worked his gaze over her beloved face. When most of the other guests had been distant to Martha, treating her as an outsider to this often-cold world of Polite Society, Emilia had engaged her daughters and also taken time to learn about the young woman. His heart shifted as he fell in love with Emilia all over again. There'd be worry enough later about the deepening intensity of that emotion. Now, he wanted to enjoy this moment—and her.

Emilia eyed him suspiciously. "Why are you looking at me like that?"

"Because I've never known a person like you in my life," he said softly.

Her lips parted. "Oh," she breathed, stirring a little cloud of white with her breath.

His gaze went to her rosebud mouth, and a hungering to take her into his arms filled him.

Nay, it had never left. It had been there, a tangible yearning he'd fought valiantly for years.

"Shall we?" she whispered, her query an invitation to claim the kiss he craved.

In a rustle of velvet, she turned dismissively and trotted over to the servants who'd continued to the stairs. As she left him staring after her retreating figure, it occurred to him that she *hadn't* been encouraging an embrace.

Of course she wasn't, you damned fool.

As Emilia spoke to the servants, Heath rubbed his chilled palms together. A moment later, the young man passed the saw over to the lady.

Marching halfway back, she held the tool aloft in Heath's direction. "Let us carry on, then."

He let his arms fall back to his sides. Earlier, he'd believed she was funning him, only to find she was dead serious. "Now?" he called over. "You wish to go tree hunting now?"

She shook her head. "No."

Heath smiled. Hunting a tree in the dead of night with snow threatening—that was the teasing he'd come to expect from the lady.

"I *am* going tree hunting now," she clarified. With that, she started down the stone steps, and he stared after her for several moments until her slender form disappeared from sight. The maid and footman followed along behind.

Yes, she intended to do this, then. This... Livonian tradition practiced by his sister-in-law and nieces and nephew. Even with servants accompanying her, Heath couldn't very well leave the lady on her own at this hour. And yet... as his legs began carrying him forward, obligation was not what had him following along. It was a need to be with her. He reached the top of the stairs and found her already twenty paces ahead, the servants trailing at a slower, shorter, more sedate pace. "You do know it is dark out, my lady?" he called after her.

"Hardly," she returned, neither breaking stride nor glancing back. "There's a full moon's glow." Her voice carried on the winter wind, echoing around the countryside.

He squinted up at the cloud-studded sky. It was more like a half-moon's much fainter glow, but that hardly merited at this point. For a second time that day, he found himself racing after the spitfire. His boots ground up snow and ice as he ran. The servants barely spared him a look as he passed.

The night chill stole the air from his lungs, so that when he reached Emilia's side, he was slightly out of breath.

With her spare hand, Emilia tipped her bonnet to the side and angled her head to look at him. "You came."

"Did you doubt I would?" he countered. With her was the only place he wanted to be. It was the only place he'd ever wanted to be. He'd been years too late, and because of that he'd lost that right.

"No, Heath." Offering him a sad smile, she held over the saw. "I knew you would come."

He tried to make sense of that, detecting layers of meaning within those five words but unable to peel back a single one of them to make any sense of.

Heading back toward the cluster of trees, he and Emilia settled into silence, the quiet broken only by the crunch of the snow. This, however, wasn't the easy quiet he'd come to appreciate these past days with her. Rather, a tension thrummed between them.

A chuckle sounded in the distance from the footman trailing far behind, the levity at odds with this newer, more stoic version of Emilia Aberdeen. Heath stole a glance back at the couple. At some point, they'd ceased walking and lingered in the background. "You've lost your servants," he noted.

"They are not my servants," she said tightly, increasing her stride and leaving Heath behind.

At some point, they'd returned to the aloofness that had long existed between them, the barriers he'd deliberately and expertly crafted. As such, he should be grateful. It certainly made it easier to honor his loyalty to Renaud.

Nay, that would never be easy. He'd go back to secretly resenting the only real friend he'd had in the world for loving the only woman Heath had ever and would ever love. Only, he wasn't grateful. There was a damned tightness in his chest over what he'd lost. *You never had her. You simply deluded yourself these past days with the lady into believing she might share the sentiments that had only been one-sided.* Sighing, he started after Emilia.

At some point, she stopped, facing an arch of fir trees. The collection of nature's artwork formed a semicircle of evergreens that had grown in ascending height.

She remained silent, her gaze locked forward, and damn him for the pathetic fool he was, but he resented blasted trees for so holding her attentions.

This was, of course, a moment that Renaud would have expertly filled with charming words. Emilia's laughter would have spilled from her lips.

God, how he hated his friend for having always possessed that ability, not for every woman, but for this one.

Say something…

"What now?" he asked and then winced, at last grateful for the absence of the glow of a full moon.

Emilia didn't even deign to look at him. "Now, we cut."

"Which one?"

She stretched a finger out, and he followed it—

Heath squinted. Perhaps he was not looking at the same fir. He leaned forward. "*Which* one?"

Emilia wagged her finger. "That one."

Yes, nothing wrong with his vision. She'd selected the tallest and fattest of the collection. He slapped the saw against his leg, contemplating the impossible task. With a sigh, he started forward.

"Very well."

Very well.

That was all he'd say?

She'd selected the largest of all the trees, a nigh impossible task for one man. And he'd not even called for the help of the servants who'd accompanied them?

Muttering under his breath, Heath doffed his hat and tossed it onto a nearby boulder. It skidded along the back of the rock and landed with a thump in the snow. As he proceeded to fall to a knee and lift the branches to inspect the trunk of the tree in question, bitterness assailed her.

That was Heath. Dutiful, obliging Heath who'd never say *no* to anyone. The same Heath who was out here even now because his mother had ordered him to occupy the poor spinster. Mayhap she'd given him a whole host of ladies to dance attendance on.

'Twas the season to spread cheer to those in need of cheering: Francesca Cornworthy, Martha... Tears clogged her throat. *Me.*

"I still say this is a silly tradition," he called into the tree's branches. He grabbed the saw.

"And yet, you'll do it a-anyway," she said, her voice shaking.

Heath paused.

"Because that is what you do. Isn't it, Heath? You come to the aid of all the poor, unfortunate souls in need of rescuing." It was wrong to resent him for being kind. Only, it wasn't that she resented his kindness. She resented his pity... She *craved* his kindness. Wanted it to be sincere and come from a place of honesty and not this lie perpetuated by him and his mother.

His back went up, and stiffening, Heath came to his feet. Slowly, he faced her. "What is this, Emilia?" he asked in grave tones.

"I don't need your pity."

He drew back as if he'd been struck. "I don't pity you."

"Oh, no? What is it one calls showing a woman a good time to cheer her up?"

Even in the cold of night, all the color drained from Heath's cheeks, leaving him pale. "Oh, God."

At least he'd not deny it. What an inconsequential consolation.

Emilia bit the inside of her lip, hating deep within her soul that he'd finally acknowledged her after all these years because of some chore he'd been given. Hating herself even more for having been duped by whatever game she herself had played and having forgotten the real motives behind his joining her. She found strength in the much safer emotion of outrage.

"Listen to me, Heath Whitworth," she hissed, striding over to him, her skirts whipping angrily about her. "I don't need you to entertain me or look after me like I'm a child." *I wanted you to want to be with me.* She jabbed a finger into his chest so hard the digit ached. "And certainly not because your mother ordered it."

The clouds shifted overhead, and a faint beam of moonlight bathed his face and illuminated the spark of hurt in Heath's dark gaze. "That is all this was, then?" he asked tiredly. "Your joining me each day was to impart some kind of lesson?"

She started.

I will not feel bad. I will not feel bad...

How dare he turn this around? "You are no different than the rest of the w-world," she whispered. It was only the cold that lent a quiver to her voice. She'd tired of the world looking at her as though all that she was, all that defined her, were the actions of another. "You look at me and see only Connell's betrayal."

Heath's throat moved wildly, but he didn't speak. What else was there for him to say?

Emilia moved so close their knees brushed, and she was forced to angle her head back to meet his gaze. "I'll have you know I found peace with what happened, and I was quite content with my life, Heath Whitworth." Emilia froze, momentarily stricken by the accidental—and worse, accurate—slip of her tense. "I *am* content," she hurriedly corrected. Too late. She'd revealed the truth she'd kept even from herself.

"Emilia," he began, but she shoved her finger into his chest once more, and he grunted.

"I already told you I do not want *anyone's* pity, Lord Heath. Not yours and not anyone's."

His expression softened, and she stumbled in her haste to put space between them.

"I don't pity you, Emilia Aberdeen," Heath's solemn utterance halted her in midstride, and she made herself stay put.

Emilia scoffed. "Come, let us not have any more lies between us. Do you truly expect me to believe that had your mother not given you specific directives to entertain me, that you would have for even one moment taken breakfast with me? Gone skating with me?" *Kissed me?* "Rescued me that evening in the billiards room?"

He briefly closed his eyes. "No, you are correct. I wouldn't have."

Her entire body jerked, and she felt like he'd run her through with that truthful admission.

Well, you sought the truth, and he gave it. "I see." There was nothing left to be said between them. Before she did something even more pathetic, such as dissolve into a blubbering mess of tears, she stomped by him.

"You don't see, Emilia," he called after her. His voice, harsh and guttural, grew increasingly closer. Emilia whipped around just as he stepped into her path and caught her by the shoulders. "You never did."

Raw emotion blazed from the depths of his eyes and seared her from the heated intensity of it.

"See what?" she managed to whisper.

Heath briefly tightened his grip upon her arms. He lowered his head so close to hers, the warmth of his breath caressed her chilled skin. "That I spent my whole life admiring you from afar." Her breath caught. "*Loving* you from afar." He abruptly released her. "So, do not think any of"—he slashed a hand between them—"*this* was because of pity or some sense of honor." With that, he stalked off.

Emilia's heart hammered against her rib cage.

Her thoughts stumbled around in circles as she sought to make sense of all he'd said… and revealed. Everything, however, twisted around in her mind, like tangled vines that could not be unwound. That revelation… his revelation defied everything she knew to be fact.

He couldn't love her.

"You do not even like me," she blurted. "You didn't know I existed."

Heath stopped and, for a long moment, remained with his back to her. "I know, Emilia. I know all too well."

But… The wind knocked her bonnet back, dislodging several strands of hair that whipped around her eyes. She slapped them back, needing an unhindered view of him. "You rarely spoke to me when I was a girl." She'd taken him for the snobbish ducal heir who'd had no need for a girl underfoot. "Why… why, you ran the other way whenever I was near."

Doffing his hat, Heath turned and faced her. "I didn't know how to be around you," he said tiredly as he fiddled with the brim. "You were spirited and playful and courageous, and I was…" He grimaced. "*Bookish* Lord Heath. Ducal heir and nothing more."

An ache settled in her chest. The person he described was what she, too, had taken him for. These past days with him, however, had shown her the parts of Heath Whitworth that she'd never looked close enough to see. Parts of him she'd come to love.

Heath cleared his throat. "I was never glib with words, and by the time I'd worked up the courage to approach you in London…" He glanced away.

"Almack's," she breathed. Her first set. He'd been the first person to dance with her when she'd made her debut.

A memory cut a swath through the tangle of weeds in her mind.

"You want to dance with me?" Emilia blurted.

Lord Heath shifted on his feet, looking as pained as he always did around her. "Unless you'd rather we not…?"

"No! I'd… like that. Very much…"

How had she not remembered that day? Nay, she recalled parts of it, including what, until this very moment, she'd erroneously believed to be the most important aspect of that day. "I…"

"Forgot?" A sad smile hovered on his lips. "And why would you recall? You met the love of your life that evening."

"And you introduced us," she whispered.

Heath chuckled, the sound devoid of even the barest hint of happiness. "I introduced you to the man who stole your heart."

Her chest ached. What would life have been like had Heath been the one who'd courted her?

As soon as the thought slid in, she hated the reality lurking alongside it: *You wouldn't have ever seen him as you do now.* She'd painted a false image of him as a proper, staid, prim lord who'd never tolerate a wife who liked to spend her summers talking with gypsies and chasing after her dreams.

She'd been so wrong about so much.

"I… I didn't know, Heath." She didn't know because he'd done such a convincing job of making her believe he didn't even like her.

He released a long sigh that stirred a soft cloud of white. "You wouldn't have," he said, jamming his hands into his cloak pockets. "Because I couldn't have you know that. My opportunity to share how I felt had come and gone."

Emilia touched a hand to her temple. It still didn't make sense. "But then, after Connell jilted me."

A muscle leaped in his jaw. "Being near you was an impossibility," he said cryptically. He exhaled slowly through his teeth. "Either way, I just thought you should know that I never disliked you. That I only ever admired your spirit and your strength."

Neither spoke for a long while, the stretch of silence agonizing.

Emilia drifted closer, and he forced himself to remain there for whatever she might say—or worse, might not say. Then she stopped and tipped her head back to meet his gaze. "*Latet enim veritas, sed nihil pretiosius veritate*," she whispered.

"Truth is hidden," he translated hoarsely, "but nothing is more beautiful than—"

Clutching the front of his cloak, Emilia kissed him.

The truth...

He stiffened as she laid claim to his mouth.

I am lost...

Or mayhap this was being found.

Groaning, he caught her hips, and with the cold winter wind assailing them, they ravaged each other's mouths, tangling their tongues in a passionate duel that burned away any remnants of the winter chill.

He caught her under her buttocks and dragged her into the vee of his legs.

Even through the fabric of her skirts, she felt his length pressed against her belly. Twining her arms about his neck, she layered her body to his in a bid to get closer. Hating the cold. Hating their garments.

She moaned and tipped her head to better take his kiss. An ache settled between her legs, agonizing and glorious at the same time.

"Emilia," he rasped against her cheek, trailing his mouth lower, his warm breath a gentle sough that drove the cold from her. Her name came over and over. In wonderment. An entreaty. A husky mark of his desire.

She tipped her head and, reaching between them, loosened the clasp at her throat, so the garment fell loose. "Heath," she returned on a keening moan as he flicked the tip of his tongue down the column of her throat before settling on that place where her pulse pounded with desire for him. And then he suckled that sensitive place.

Emilia bit her cheek to keep from crying out. "Mmmm," she whimpered.

She was afire. A spark had ignited, and the conflagration now consumed her. "I'll never be cold again," she panted.

Thwack.

Snow fell from her brow and blurred her vision. Teeth chattering, Emilia wiped the remnants away.

Together, she and Heath looked up to the evergreen branch overhead that quivered in the aftermath of dropping a mound of snow atop them.

"H-holy h-hell," she managed. "I-I was wrong." She was deuced freezing.

Catching her to him, Heath drew her close and held her.

Their chests shook with a shared giddy amusement.

"Are we still cutting d-down th-that tree, m-my lady?"

Emilia wrapped her arms around his waist, and clinging to him, she glanced back so she could meet his gaze. "M-mayhap we wait until it is lighter and a wee bit warmer."

Nonetheless, Emilia and Heath remained there in the cold, holding each other. With his arms wound about her, his embrace felt like… home.

CHAPTER 12

*A gentleman who believes a lady should not have
dreams outside of him and his happiness is not a
gentleman worth marrying.*
Mrs. Matcher
A Lady's Guide to a Gentleman's Heart

THE CHRISTMASTIDE SEASON MUST BE a time of miracles, after all. Because for the first time in the whole of his life, Heath didn't want one of his mother's usually infernal house parties to end.

He wanted the event to continue on.

Nay, that wasn't altogether true.

He wanted his time with Emilia to continue on.

Since their time together under the firs, when he'd confessed all, each moment of each day had been filled with a joy he'd not believed possible. Joy he'd never known. Because of her.

Only…

You didn't confess all… There was one key fact you carefully omitted from your telling.

In the moments when that reminder slid in, along with it came a deserved guilt. He'd sought to ease his conscience by telling himself that Renaud's secret wasn't for him to share. That he had an obligation to keep that confidence close.

Yet, he recognized the selfishness in that.

"What of this one?" Emilia's voice cut briefly across his musings.

She deserved the truth from him, because otherwise, all this joy they had found together now was predicated on a lie. "Splendid," he forced himself to say. He wound a thread of berries around the garland he'd begun making with Emilia several hours earlier.

"Perhaps if I place this one here?" she was asking.

I don't want this moment with her to end... I want... her. Nay, us. I want us to have a future, together. "Splendid," he said again. Because everything she did was nothing short of it.

Emilia shifted closer to him on the workbench, and he stiffened. "Here we are, then," she murmured, tucking a tangle of berries behind his ear.

He blinked slowly.

Emilia grazed her fingertips along his chin, bringing his eyes to hers. "You weren't paying attention, were you?"

"I confess my mind was elsewhere."

She grinned. "La, sir, you know how to flatter a lady."

Actually, she was right with that jest. He was rubbish at it, which was what had seen him to this point.

Her smile slipped. Setting down the embellishments in her hands, she slid her palm atop his hand, twining their fingers. "I was teasing, Heath," she said gently.

Forcing back the mountain of regrets and the ghost of Renaud, Heath refocused his energies on her... and this moment.

Leaning close, she tugged his lapels, bringing him closer. "Though I admit," she whispered against his mouth, "you do wear holly berries well."

"Minx," he muttered, taking her lips in a quick kiss, wanting to explore those supple contours further. Alas... He glanced about for the pair of servants who were never far from any activity he and Emilia took part in.

"They are not around," she tempted, lifting her lips once more.

He swallowed, battling himself. "They might return at any moment." Even as he knew that, the urge to taste her was an even greater temptation than that succulent fruit Adam had traded his soul for. He kissed her.

"They won't," she promised when he again ended their kiss. "They are otherwise occupied."

As they always were, with some task or another she gave to Stanley and the Scottish girl, Isla.

"They are in love."

He cocked his head.

"They're smitten with one another, and so…" Her eyes twinkled with mischief.

"And so you invite them along as absentee chaperones."

Emilia tapped her index finger to the tip of his nose. "*Precisely.*" She went back to winding the strand of beads around the length of garland.

"Why…" Heath opened and closed his mouth several times. "You are playing *matchmaker.*"

"Incorrect," she clarified, clipping out each of those three syllables. She reached the end of the greenery and knotted off the end of her beads. "I *played* matchmaker." A pleased grin curled her lips into a wide smile. "Stanley asked her to marry him." The announcement had an almost wistful quality.

He sank back in his seat. Was there nothing she couldn't do? "How…?"

"I'd noted the way they stole glances at one another. They simply required, and deserved, time to be with one another. And the rest?" She lifted her shoulders in a little shrug. "It came together when they had the opportunity to *be* together." Emilia's eyes grew distant. "How singularly odd."

He roamed his eyes over her face. "What?"

"That I should see it so clearly in others and yet failed to see…" He trailed the pad of his thumb along her lower lip. The flesh trembled under his caress, and she looked at him, then her long golden lashes swept low. "*You* and everything you were feeling."

Heath drew his hand back. "It is oftentimes easier to see in others what might not be so clear in one's own circumstances."

They resumed working on their garland until Emilia hesitated, toying with her strand of beads. "I've something to… share with you."

He set aside his greenery and waited.

Swinging a leg over the bench, she matched his position. Only… straddling the bench as she was, her skirts rucked about her ankles and mid-calves, revealed the well-muscled limbs that were a product of a woman skilled at riding.

She pinched him.

"Ouch," he muttered. "What in blazes was that for?"

"You aren't paying attention."

Heath bristled. "I certainly was." He had been. Mayhap just not to what she'd intended.

"To my pink stockings." As if there were another pair in question, the lady pointed at her slippers.

Heath's gaze fell lower, and heat wound its way through his veins as an erotic image played in his mind of him stripping each sheer, shimmery article from her shapely calves. Winding them lower. One at a time. "Oww."

"You were doing it again, and I am trying to confess something to you."

That penetrated the haze of lust. His mouth went dry as he braced for the declaration he'd hungered for—

"I'm Mrs. Matcher."

She was... and then it was not the surname that registered, but rather, the form of address before it. "You are... married?" His stomach muscles twisted. Only Emilia Aberdeen would secretly wed, and Heath was riddled with a blinding rage to end—

"Do stop. I am not married." A relief so vast swept through him that it brought his eyes briefly closed. She gave him a slight shove. "I am Mrs. *Matcher*," she repeated, as if that should mean something to him.

He shook his head slowly. "I am afraid I am not following."

"It is a column in the *London Post*. I provide guidance to men and women on how to snare the heart of their beloved. Quite scandalous, isn't it? A lady paid for her work."

Yes, her mother and his mother and all of Polite Society would be horrified at the mere prospect of it. He peered at her and saw the telltale nervousness in her expressive eyes, the tension at the corners of her mouth. She expected him to take exception to her... revelation. A revelation she'd shared with no one before him.

"How long have you been the infamous Mrs. Matcher?" he asked, yearning to know every secret she carried.

"After—" *Renaud*. "After Connell jilted me, I despised leaving home. Everyone would stare, and everyone was talking about me and that day."

"And so you began reading everything you could find." That was when she'd taught herself Latin.

She brightened. "Precisely. I tortured myself by reading all the gossip columns." They'd been riddled with her and Renaud's names. Heath had despised those pages for raking her name through them. "And I came upon a column in the *Post*. It offered advice to ladies seeking the heart of a gentleman, and it was full of such rubbish, I penned a lengthy letter, informing the editor in no fewer than one hundred and twenty-six terms of everything wrong with that section."

He grinned, imagining the expression of that nameless man as he'd been ripped into by the indefatigable Emilia Aberdeen. "I trust he was offended?"

"Oh, no, not at all. He hired me. It was but seven hundred words each post, and yet, it gave me purpose, and it taught me that which I'd failed to understand until that point."

"And what was that?"

"That I didn't want to marry. That I didn't want a husband. Writing my column brought me a contentment and was safe in ways that loving was... is dangerous. I receive a pittance for the work I do, and the number of words I write each week is small, but it is something that belongs to me and something I'd be expected to give up were I to marry." She spoke so matter-of-factly, with a pride and self-confidence in herself and the work she did, that he fell in love with her all over again.

He cupped her cheek, the skin silken smooth and warm under his touch. "Who is to say you cannot have both, Emilia?"

"Society," she said instantly.

"Any gentleman who'd expect you to sacrifice any part of yourself is no man worthy of you."

Her breath caught in a little inhalation. "I've not scandalized you, then?"

He gathered the scissors, snipped the top of a pink rose from the overflowing urn, and tucked it behind her ear. "Are you disappointed that I'm not?"

Emilia brushed her fingertips against the bloom, and then, gripping Heath by his jacket, she dragged him down for a kiss. "No," she whispered, breathless, as she released him. "It makes me love you all the more, Heath Whitworth."

It makes her love him all the more?

He went absolutely still. Afraid to move. Afraid to shatter the moment and find that he'd merely dreamed that utterance from her lips.

Emilia shifted onto her knees and then sank back so they were perfectly eye to eye. "I love you, Heathcliff Whitworth."

It was everything he'd yearned to hear and not allowed himself even a dream of. Those five words, that vow and his name, filled every corner of his being with a lightness.

Gathering her hands in his, he kissed first one and then the other. "The guests will be arising soon."

These were their stolen moments away from the busybodies who craved gossip and would intrude on this newfound relationship Emilia and Heath had found with each other.

Emilia's lips pulled. "Yes, they have a tendency to do that, don't they?"

I don't want this to be a secret. But... neither could there truly be anything between them until the past was sorted out.

"You're looking melancholy again, Heathcliff," she murmured. Going up on her knees, she placed her lips close to his ear. "Do you know what they say helps with that?" she breathed, bathing his senses with the hint of peppermint.

You. You chase away all the darkness. She always had. "What do they say?" he croaked.

"Cutting down the holiday tree." She winked.

He chuckled. "Minx." He caught her lips in a quick kiss. *Hell. You're going to hell for betraying the only friend you've ever had.* Heath forced himself to relinquish her mouth. "It is still snowing." Their intentions to return for the holiday tree had been waylaid by the unrelenting storm that had blanketed the grounds.

"Pfft," she scoffed. "It is slowed to a near stop."

After three days of snow, the drives and paths and roads would all be covered. Heath tucked a loose golden curl behind her ear. "Fetch your lovebirds."

A twinkle lit her eyes.

"I'll meet you at the end of the drive," he whispered, stealing another kiss.

Rapid footfalls echoed from outside the conservatory. "Oh, bloody hell," he whispered.

"For the love of goodness sake, Heath, you had better be in there." The frustrated utterance sounded from the corridor. "Or

I'll sack the servants you'd have hide your whereabouts from me."

"You need to go," he mouthed. Tossing his jacket around her shoulders, he guided her to the glass doors that led outside.

"There's something wicked to these clandestine meetings." She giggled, hurrying off.

He quietly opened the doors. "The next door—"

"I know my way about, and I'm hardly afraid of snow."

With that, she darted off, slipping and sliding along the shoveled terrace, which was slick from the remnants of snow that coated the surface. He followed her flight, confirming that she'd reached the door.

She darted a hand up, waving at him, and as entranced as he'd always been, he stole another wave just as his mother burst into the conservatory.

"There you are!" she squawked, her chest heaving from her exertions, her cheeks flushed. "I have been searching everywhere for you," she panted. "What…?" She blinked wildly. "What are you doing?" she blurted, glancing at the partially open doors out to the terrace.

Reluctantly, he drew the doors closed. "Nothing." He'd not been made for subterfuge. "What emergency has struck now?" he drawled, strolling back to the worktable in a bid to stymie her questions.

Except, taking up a spot beside the two strands of garland only brought his mother's focus to those ornaments. She picked one up and studied the gold beads. "Why… why… are you making garland?"

He swallowed a sigh. "I promised Creda and Iris I'd join them later to decorate." Which wasn't an untruth. He, however, had chosen to step around the fact that he and Emilia had made those strands. "I trust you've not come to speak with me about my duties as uncle."

His mother abruptly released the decoration Emilia had been working on. "No." The color slipped from her cheeks, leaving her pale. "There is a problem," she whispered. "Renaud is here."

There was a humming in his ears. He'd heard her wrong. Surely. The young duke didn't leave his Cornwall estates. "Renaud?"

His mother nodded.

He shook his head.

"Connell," she repeated and then wrung her hands together. "Your friend. Emilia's former betrothed."

The muscles of his stomach knotted from the tension that whipped through him. "I know who Renaud is."

"Then why did you ask me?" she cried softly, tossing her hands up.

Renaud, who remained closed away from the rest of the world, had emerged from hiding and come *here*? For what end?

Except, as soon as the question slipped in, the answer was close behind.

For her.

It had been only a matter of time.

His heart fell and sank like a stone in his belly. "Renaud is here," he said, his voice flat to his own ears, still unable to completely process. "He's here *now*. What does he want?" He already knew. Already feared...

She eyed him with heartbreak in her eyes. "He is asking to see Lady Emilia."

Just like that, all the light and warmth went out of him. This was the moment of inevitability, the reunion long overdue between young loves, that would see Heath forever cut from Emilia's life.

"What exactly is it that you expect of me?" he asked hollowly.

His mother frowned. "Well, I think it should be obvious."

Actually, no, it wasn't. Nothing was. Everything was turned upside down.

With an exaggerated sigh, she filled each hand with the two incomplete strands of garland and, giving them a pointed look, arched an eyebrow. "Do you truly think that I believe you were here alone making garland, Heathcliff Whitworth?" she chided.

He squirmed. Yes, it would be foolish to expect his far-too-astute mother to fail to note just where he'd been these past three days, and with whom.

Releasing the garland, his mother rested a hand on his. "Was I mistaken in thinking you might... care for Emilia?" she asked gently. "Mayhap even love her?"

He dragged a hand over his face. All of her efforts at this house party had been with the intention of playing matchmaker.

His mother touched his arm. "Was I... Am I... mistaken?" she pressed.

"You weren't. You aren't," he said tiredly and sank down onto the workbench he and Emilia had occupied... moments ago? A lifetime ago? Time had ceased to mean anything or matter in any way.

His mother fell onto the seat beside him. "Then you need to... do something."

Do something? "What does that even mean, Mother?"

"Fight for her."

"He is the man she loves." Even saying that ripped a ragged hole inside his already breaking heart.

"Loved," she amended. "And he betrayed her," she tacked on. "Betrayed her, Heathcliff. *Betraaaaayed* her." She stretched her hands out to emphasize those elongated syllables.

His mother spoke of feelings Emilia had had long ago. Except, any resentment Emilia had harbored over the years had been because she didn't know the reasons for that betrayal.

"Won't you say something, Heath?"

"What is there to say?" *That I love Emilia and losing her again will shatter me beyond repair and leave me eternally empty inside.* "He had his reasons," he said tiredly. Ones only Heath knew of. Ones that were honorable, and yet, never could be explained because of what that would mean for so many.

His mother gasped. "You would *defend* him? I know he is your dearest friend, but you would simply allow him to sweep in here all these years later and win her back?"

His throat worked. "I want her to be happy." He wanted to know she was loved and that she lived a life of joy... even if that meant she was with another.

His mother settled an arm around his shoulders and lightly squeezed. "*You* make her happy, Heathcliff. I've known Emilia since she was a babe, and I saw her with Renaud. She was never like she is when she is with you."

He started. "How—?"

Her eyes sparkled. "A mother knows her child, Heathcliff. Just as a mother knows when a woman is in love with her child. Go fight for her," she urged.

Go fight for her...

It was a primal urging to fight that reared deep inside him. Only... "It is not that simple." He shoved to his feet and began pacing. He wanted a life with Emilia. He wanted her to want that life with him. It was not, however, his place to interfere in her relationship with Renaud. He stopped abruptly and stared at the doorway. "Where is he?"

"Your father hid him in his office. He's refused to allow him out." For the first time since she'd stormed the conservatory, a smile pulled his mother's lips up. "He's occupying him with his snuffbox collection."

Were Heath's world not crumbling about him, he'd have laughed uproariously at the idea of his father serving as sentry with snuff-boxes as his weaponry of choice.

There was only one thing, however, he could do.

Heath started for the door.

"What are you going to do?"

He didn't break stride. "The right thing." His heart breaking, Heath wound his way through his family's estate. The same corridors he and Emilia had stolen down these past days together. Emotion stuck in his throat. Damn it all.

At last, he reached his father's office and froze with his fingers on the handle. "...and this particular box was gifted to Nelson by his personal secretary, Unwin," his father was saying. "I have it on good authority—"

Heath let himself in, and it was hard to say who was more relieved to see him—his father or Renaud.

"That particular box was gifted during a dinner party in Sicily in '98," Heath finished.

"It is good to know someone listens around here." His father thumped the desk in a primal mark of paternal approval.

"Father, may I have a moment?" he asked quietly.

The older duke was already moving out from behind the desk. Not bothering with a parting greeting, he paused alongside Heath. "Your mother will hang me by my feet if you allow that one free reign of these halls."

Yes, Heath's mother was nothing if not loyal. Loyalty seemed to be the bane of the Whitworth existence.

"And another thing"—his father tossed a suspicious look over at Renaud—"watch my snuffboxes around that one. Don't trust a gent who won't honor his word."

When his father had gone, Heath closed the door and stared at the panel for a moment, unable to face his friend.

"You needn't feel badly about that. I quite deserved it," his friend called over in somber tones that brought Heath around to face him.

No, but there were all manner of other things he did and should feel horrid over. Betrayals that spoke to Heath's blackened soul. "You're here," he said needlessly.

"It is overdue," Renaud said, glancing around the office. A small smile formed on his lips, though sad and empty. "Nothing has changed here, I see," he murmured, directing that to the duke's snuffbox collection.

Everything had changed here.

"My parents are insistent that you leave," Heath said, tired of sidestepping the reason for his friend's visit.

Renaud's shoulders came back. "And what of you, Mulgrave?" he returned, coming to the middle of the carpet. Suspicion darkened his friend's life-hardened gaze. "What do you want?"

Heath fisted and unfisted his hands. For, God rot his soul, he wanted Emilia. He wanted Renaud gone. And he wanted to go back to the joy he'd known with Emilia. Heath met the man he'd known since Eton in the middle of the room. "It's been ten *years*, Renaud."

A muscle ticked at the corner of the duke's right eye. "I don't need you to tell me how long it's been since I've seen her." He took another step toward Heath. "Just as I don't intend to let your parents"—he gave Heath a hard look—"or you prevent me from seeing Emilia because of some misbegotten fear of what the *ton* will say about our meeting."

He started past Heath.

"Before you do, there's something I'd say to you," he said after Emilia's former betrothed.

The duke stopped and wheeled slowly around. "What is it?"

Nihil durat in aeternum…Nothing lasts forever…

CHAPTER 13

All you need is love. That is, the love of a good,
honorable gentleman.
Mrs. Matcher
A Lady's Guide to a Gentleman's Heart

ON THE MORNING OF HER wedding, when she'd been in her full bridal regalia and on her way to meet her bridegroom, her carriage had been stopped midway through the journey to the cathedral. That was when a servant of the Duke of Renaud delivered the note that had changed the rest of her life.

From that moment on, Emilia had learned to brace herself when something unexpected happened.

That was why, as she stood outside and caught sight of Barry striding down the steps of Lady Sutton's terrace with a hunting rifle in hand and their mother following close behind, unease formed in her belly.

"Where is he?" Barry demanded, his impressive display of fury ruined as he reached the bottom step and skidded on ice.

The rifle tumbled from his fingers.

"Barry," their mother cried. "Have a care with that." Yes, their mother would be panicked at the possibility of any accident befalling the Gayle heir. "You are going to require that shot."

Emilia's stomach churned. Bloody hell, this was bad indeed. Of all damned times for her brother to become a protective sort. "I assure you both," she said in even tones, "that I'm quite old enough to make decisions for myself."

Her brother inspected the chambers of his weapon. "Oh, with all due respect reserved for someone of your advanced years, I couldn't care less about what you want," he informed her quite cheerily. "This is more about what the gentleman deserves."

Squinting, Barry aimed the gun at the terrace.

Growling, Emilia gripped the weapon and forced it sideways until the barrel pointed safely at the ground. "I've had enough of your theatrics. I am here because I want to be here."

Her mother released a shuddery gasp and pressed her fingertips to her lips. "You do not know what you are saying."

How could they continue to judge him still? "I know very well what manner of man he is, Mother. And he deserves far more than this treatment."

"Your father and his blasted gout," Mother muttered to herself. "He leaves me to deal with all this."

Emilia pursed her mouth. "I beg your pardon?"

"Your judgment has been forever flawed where gentlemen are concerned, Emilia Aberdeen," her mother charged, giving a toss of her hair. The plait her maid had clearly not had time to tend flopped over her shoulder. "Well, since your father couldn't bring himself to be here, I'll make the decision." *The decision?* Her mother turned to Barry. "You have my permission to shoot him."

"You are impossible," she cried out, throwing her palms up in the air. "He is all that is good and—" Her gaze collided with that of the tall figure overhead. "Oh," she whispered. They hadn't been speaking about Heath.

But for the wind whisking through the countryside, only silence met her utterance.

Early on, after his defection, all of her thoughts of the Duke of Renaud had come with rage and hurt. In time, her feelings had shifted, and she'd wondered who he'd become. She'd wondered, given the way she had been forever altered by the way their betrothal ended, if he too had changed.

Standing here before her now, he was a stranger... in so many ways.

More muscular and broader across the shoulders, he had a raw, bearlike quality to him different than the strapping rogue who'd caught her eye and then her heart. His hair, always unfashionably long, now hung even longer past his neck. Gone was the half grin he'd worn as effortlessly as his own skin. In its place was a somber, terse line of hard lips.

In the end, the likeliest of their quartet broke the impasse. The duchess stepped between her daughter and the man who'd broken her heart a lifetime ago. "Leave this instant, Renaud. My daughter has nothing to say to you—"

Emilia rested a hand on her mother's arm. "Mama," she murmured, but her mother continued over that interruption.

"—now or e—"

"Mother," she repeated in firmer tones that at last penetrated her mother's diatribe.

Renaud started down the steps.

Barry shifted so he stood shoulder to shoulder with Emilia.

At last, he reached the assembled Aberdeens.

In the earliest days of being jilted, Emilia had thought about what would happen when she again saw Connell. She'd alternated between scripting hateful invectives and pleading for him to love her as she'd loved him.

But now, all these years later, there was a peculiar... nothingness to this meeting. This man with a distant, impenetrable stare was, and always had been, a stranger. The time they'd shared had been thrilling and exciting, but also... empty. She'd not allowed him to see the hopes she'd carried, because at that point, she'd been a girl who hadn't yet known what those hopes were.

Unlike Heath. Heath, who didn't eye her as a peculiarity for speaking Latin, but rather, conversed with her in those foreign tongues. Heath, with whom she was capable of laughing. Heath, in whom she'd freely confided the work she'd done and received no recrimination.

"Emilia," Connell finally said, removing his hat as he did.

Her brother raised his hunting rifle as if the man opposite him had just declared war.

"I'll have a moment with His Grace." Emilia issued the directive without taking her gaze from her former betrothed.

"Are you sure you'd not rather I shoot him?" Barry offered. "I'm a far better shot than when I was as a boy."

Going up on tiptoe, Emilia kissed his cheek. "*Go.*"

Her younger brother glared menacingly at the stoically immo-bile duke before allowing the duchess to tug him along. Emilia's devoted kin reached the top of the stairs, and each sent one last scowl at the duke before disappearing.

Emilia stared at her former love. What did one say after all these years?

There was a certainty that, of anyone, this charming, affable rogue would be the first with a word, and it would always be the right one.

Only...

She peered at him.

He no longer had those words. Just as she'd been changed, so too had Connell been marked by the passage of time and life.

"This meeting is overdue, Emilia," he finally said, tapping his hat against his leg, the only hint that he was uneasy in this meeting.

"Yes," she said simply. "Yes, it is." Years overdue.

"I should have called upon you."

"There was a lot you should have done, Connell." She paused. "And just as much you shouldn't have done."

The jilting.

Except... had he not jilted her, they'd even now be married, and Heath would have remained a stranger, and Emilia would have never discovered herself... and the man who filled her life in ways she'd not previously realized she was missing.

Connell roamed his gaze over her face before wandering over. "No. I shouldn't have left you. I owed you the truth."

The truth...

He stared at his hat for a moment, flexing the stiff brim. "Two years before we met, I was named guardian to a young woman. I was just twenty and far more interested in my own pleasures and pursuits than in caring for the orphaned daughter of my late father."

In this telling, her former betrothed unveiled another part of himself that had been a secret. "You never mentioned her."

"I wouldn't have," he said tersely. "My obligations were met financially, and the fact that a sixteen-year-old charge had been placed in my care didn't at first concern a young man wholly besotted."

Besotted.

Yes, she could see now that that was the correct word to capture what she—what they—had felt for each other. As a young woman who'd just made her Come Out, however, there had been only the excitement to be found in a whirlwind courtship with a gentleman more exciting than any other she'd known before him.

"And… this young woman," she ventured. "She is the reason you broke off our betrothal." A legal contract that, had her family pursued it, would have seen Connell answer to the law for violating the arrangement.

"She is the reason," he said quietly. "The night prior to our wedding, I learned a dastard had taken advantage of her." Emilia didn't move. As Connell went on with his telling, there was a rote quality to his voice, as if he'd divorced himself from his connection to their long-ago relationship. "The young lady was painfully shy and trusting and… innocent. And during my time in London, I was wholly preoccupied with my own happiness." He paused and glanced at Emilia.

He was speaking of Emilia.

"Because of that," he resumed in the same grave tones, "I failed to properly look after the young woman. She found herself with child. And I found myself… with new responsibilities."

He hadn't trusted her. He had either believed her incapable of standing beside him through the heartbreak his sister had endured, or hadn't cared enough to have Emilia stand beside him and his family.

"There are no excuses for my having simply left. I was young, and yet, that is not an excuse. At the time, I made what I felt was the only decision I could make." His eyes glinted with sadness. "It is a decision I would make again. But I would have told you before I left. That is the difference, Emilia."

Shivering, Emilia folded her arms and turned away, rubbing to bring warmth to the chilled limbs. He'd abandoned her to save another. Her heart wrenched for the young woman who'd known pain. What suffering the lady had known. And on the heels of that, there was something else… "You didn't trust that I would stand beside you and your ward?"

His expression revealed nothing. "I made the decision I thought best at the time."

In short, his was a non-answer that said everything and nothing all at the same time—he'd never seen her as his partner in life. What future could she truly have had with a man who'd been unable to confide in her? A man whose opinion of her had been so low that he'd not trusted she'd have been there for him? To Connell, she'd been a pretty ornament. Whereas Heath? Heath listened to her, and spoke with her and to her about her dreams and beliefs. "Why should you tell me this now?" Why, when he hadn't trusted her enough to tell her then?

"I thought we might… begin again," he said quietly, his voice coming just over her shoulder.

She weighed her response a moment. "Why?" she asked curiously, glancing back. Why, when nothing in his tone or words bespoke love or even fondness?

"Because I wronged you."

Guilt.

"Because I loved you," he added as an almost secondary afterthought.

Loved. As in formerly and no more. He didn't love her. Not truly. Perhaps he had all those years ago. Or perhaps he hadn't. Either way, there was only one certainty: He was not her future. He never had been.

"Oh, Connell," she murmured, bringing herself to face him. "A lifetime has passed since I was that girl at Almack's and you were the one squiring me about London. It was exciting. We were young loves, hopelessly infatuated, but now?" she added gently. "We're both entirely different people." He was a shadow of his former self… just as she'd been. Until this house party. Until Heath had reminded her what it was to smile and laugh and love again.

"You no longer love me," he said flatly, giving the first indication that her change in feelings might matter to him.

She'd no wish to hurt him, and yet neither could she withhold the truth from him. "I fell in love with another."

He tensed. "Who?"

Emilia hesitated. This was Heath's best friend. She'd no wish to be the divide between them, and yet there had been too many mistruths between all of them. "It is Heath."

Connell gave no outward indication he'd heard her. And then, he spoke. "Heath?"

She nodded once.

"I...see."

What did he see? His gaze was dark and hard and empty.

"I love him," she said softly.

Her former betrothed rocked on his heels. "He makes you happy?"

"He does." Heath had brought her more joy than she'd ever believed herself capable of.

"I see," he repeated, in those deadened tones that hammered home the indefatigable truth: He was a stranger. Connell knocked his hat against his leg and then placed it atop his head. He remained silent for a long while. Lingering as if he wished to say more. And young girl that she'd once been, Emilia would have traded her soul to hear words of love from his lips. The woman she'd become had found happiness and love...with another. Connell abruptly stopped that distracted tap. "I wish you every happiness, Emilia." Sketching a bow, he left.

Emilia remained where she was long after he'd gone.

It was done.

And there was something freeing in his having at last come. Retying the strings of her bonnet, Emilia made the long climb to the terrace—and froze at the top of the steps.

Heath stood there, sans jacket, just as she'd left him in the conservatory.

"Renaud came," he said.

"He did," she said needlessly, hating that he wore a stone mask that she could not read. Her family and his family would have all sent Renaud to the devil if they'd had their way. "You sent him to me." It was a prediction she knew to be fact before he even gave the slight nod of confirmation. "Why?" she asked, drifting over to him.

"Because I knew," he said quietly. "I knew that his reasons and decisions long ago, though... faulty, were also honorable."

Honorable. Heath was the singularly most honorable person she'd ever known, and as such, he'd kept Connell's confidence and had also been willing to turn her over to another. The thought sent agony sluicing through her. "And so you'd just... l-let me g-go," she stammered, the tremble to her voice a product of cold and hurt.

Heath walked toward her and stopped once only a handbreadth

separated them. "Before I sent Renaud to you, I told him that I love you, but I also knew how you both felt toward one another." His chest heaved with the force of his emotion. "I vowed to him that I'd not be the man who stood between you and your happiness, Emilia." His face spasmed. "Because even as it would cost me my heart losing you, I'd not have you on a lie. I'd not even have you if it ensured my happiness, because the only joy I can know is if you are happ—"

Emilia kissed him into silence. "I love y-you," she whispered, her voice breaking. She captured his beloved face between her gloved hands. "You infuriatingly loyal, honorable, clever, witty man. I love *you.*"

Joy and disbelief together glinted in his eyes. "But—"

Emilia kissed him again, willing him to feel all the love she carried and would only ever carry for him. "I love you, and you shan't talk me out of it."

Heath wrapped his arms around her and held tight. "And swift," he breathed between kisses. "Do not forget I'm swift of foot."

She laughed, mirth shaking her frame. "You insufferable corkbrain."

All amusement faded.

Heath sank to a knee.

Emilia gasped.

"Now, *him* I approve of."

As one, Emilia and Heath looked to the doors where Barry and her parents stood alongside Heath's parents.

"Hush this instance, Barry Aberdeen," their mother clipped out, catching him by the ear and dragging him from view.

The group immediately dissolved.

Emilia's lips twitched. "You were saying, my lord?"

"Marry me, Emilia Aberdeen. And if you do, I pledge—"

She hurled herself into his arms, knocking him flat. With a grunt, he went down hard on the stone terrace. "I don't need you to make any promises or offerings," she breathed against his mouth, "but one."

"Anything," he said automatically, holding her close.

Emilia caressed her fingertips over his lips. "*Amor aeternus.*"

His throat moved. "Love forever," he whispered.

As he took her into his arms, Emilia tasted that promise in his kiss.

THE END

OTHER BOOKS BY
CHRISTI CALDWELL

THE ROGUE WHO RESCUED HER
Book 3 in the "Brethren" Series by Christi Caldwell

Martha Donaldson went from being a nobleman's wife, and respected young mother, to the scandal of her village. After learning the dark lie perpetuated against her by her 'husband', she knows better than to ever trust a man. Her children are her life and she'll protect them at all costs. When a stranger arrives seeking the post of stable master, everything says to turn him out. So why does she let him stay?

Lord Sheldon Graham Whitworth has lived with the constant reminders of his many failings. The third son of a duke, he's long been underestimated: that however, proves a valuable asset as he serves the Brethren, an illustrious division in the Home Office. When Graham's first mission sees him assigned the role of guard to a young widow and her son, he wants nothing more than to finish quickly and then move on to another, more meaningful assignment.

Except, as the secrets between them begin to unravel, Martha's trust is shattered, and Graham is left with the most vital mission he'll ever face—winning Martha's heart.

The Lady Who Loved Him
Book 2 in the "Brethren" Series by Christi Caldwell

In this passionate, emotional Regency romance by Christi Caldwell, society's most wicked rake meets his match in the clever Lady Chloe Edgerton! And nothing will ever be the same!

She doesn't believe in marriage....

The cruelty of men is something Lady Chloe Edgerton understands. Even in her quest to better her life and forget the past, men always seem determined to control her. Overhearing the latest plan to wed her to a proper gentleman, Chloe finally has enough...but one misstep lands her in the arms of the most notorious rake in London.

The Marquess of Tennyson doesn't believe in love....

Leopold Dunlop is a ruthless, coldhearted rake... a reputation he has cultivated. As a member of The Brethren, a secret spy network, he's committed his life to serving the Crown, but his rakish reputation threatens to overshadow that service. When he's caught in a compromising position with Chloe, it could be the last nail in the coffin of his career unless he's willing to enter into a marriage of convenience.

A necessary arrangement...

A loveless match from the start, it soon becomes something more. As Chloe and Leo endeavor to continue with the plans for their lives prior to their marriage, Leo finds himself not so immune to his wife – or to the prospect of losing her.

The Spy Who Seduced Her
Book 1 in the "Brethren" Series by Christi Caldwell

A widow with a past... The last thing Victoria Barrett, the Viscountess Waters, has any interest in is romance. When the only man she's ever loved was killed she endured an arranged marriage to a cruel man in order to survive. Now widowed, her only focus is on clearing her son's name from the charge of murder. That is until the love of her life returns from the grave.

A leader of a once great agency… Nathaniel Archer, the Earl of Exeter head of the Crown's elite organization, The Brethren, is back on British soil. Captured and tortured 20 years ago, he clung to memories of his first love until he could escape. Discovering she has married whilst he was captive, Nathaniel sets aside the distractions of love…until an unexpected case is thrust upon him—to solve the murder of the Viscount Waters. There is just one complication: the prime suspect's mother is none other than Victoria, the woman he once loved with his very soul.

Secrets will be uncovered and passions rekindled. Victoria and Nathaniel must trust one another if they hope to start anew—in love and life. But will duty destroy their last chance?

ROGUES RUSH IN
A Regency Duet by Tessa Dare & Christi Caldwell

New York Times and *USA Today* Bestselling authors Tessa Dare and Christi Caldwell come together in this smart, sexy, not-to-be-missed Regency Duet!

Two scandalous brides…
Two rogues who won't be denied…
His Bride for the Taking by NYT Bestselling author Tessa Dare
It's the first rule of friendship among gentlemen: Don't even think about touching your best friend's sister. But Sebastian, Lord Byrne, has never been one for rules. He's thought about touching Mary Clayton—a lot—and struggled to resist temptation. But when Mary's bridegroom leaves her waiting at the altar, only Sebastian can save her from ruin. By marrying her himself.

In eleven years, he's never laid a finger on his best friend's sister. Now he's going to take her with both hands. To have, to hold… and to love.

His Duchess for a Day by USA Today Bestseller Christi Caldwell
It was never meant to be…

That's what Elizabeth Terry has told herself while trying to forget the man she married—her once best friend. Passing herself off as a widow, Elizabeth has since built a life for herself as an instructor at a finishing school, far away from that greatest of mistakes. But the past has a way of finding you, and now that her husband has found her, Elizabeth must face the man she's tried to forget.

It was time to right a wrong…

Crispin Ferguson, the Duke of Huntington, has spent the past years living with regret. The young woman he married left without a by-your-leave, and his hasty elopement had devastating repercussions. Despite everything, Crispin never stopped thinking about Elizabeth. Now that he's found her, he has one request—be his duchess, publicly, just for a day.

Can spending time together as husband and wife rekindle the bond they once shared? Or will a shocking discovery tear them apart…this time, forever?

THE VIXEN

Book 2 in the "Wicked Wallflowers" Series by Christi Caldwell

Set apart by her ethereal beauty and fearless demeanor, Ophelia Killoran has always been a mystery to those around her—and a woman they underestimated. No one would guess that she spends her nights protecting the street urchins of St. Giles. Ophelia knows what horrors these children face. As a young girl, she faced those horrors herself, and she would have died…if not for the orphan boy who saved her life.

A notorious investigator, Connor Steele never expected to encounter Ophelia Killoran on his latest case. It has been years since he sacrificed himself for her. Now, she hires orphans from the street to work in her brother's gaming hell. But where does she find the children…and what are her intentions?

Ophelia and Connor are at odds. After all, Connor now serves the nobility, and that is a class of people Ophelia knows first-hand not to trust. But if they can set aside their misgivings and work together, they may discover that their purposes—and their hearts—are perfectly aligned.

THE HELLION
Book 1 in the "Wicked Wallflowers" Series by Christi Caldwell

Adair Thorne has just watched his gaming-hell dream disappear into a blaze of fire and ash, and he's certain that his competitors, the Killorans, are behind it. His fury and passion burn even hotter when he meets Cleopatra Killoran, a tart-mouthed vixen who mocks him at every turn. If she were anyone else but the enemy, she'd ignite a desire in him that would be impossible to control.

No one can make Cleopatra do anything. That said, she'll do whatever it takes to protect her siblings—even if that means being sponsored by their rivals for a season in order to land a noble husband. But she will not allow her head to be turned by the infuriating and darkly handsome Adair Thorne.

There's only one thing that threatens the rules of the game: Cleopatra's secret. It could unravel the families' tenuous truce and shatter the unpredictably sinful romance mounting between the hellion…and a scoundrel who could pass for the devil himself.

TO TEMPT A SCOUNDREL
Book 15 in the "Heart of a Duke" Series by Christi Caldwell

Never trust a gentleman…

Once before, Lady Alice Winterbourne trusted her heart to an honorable, respectable man… only to be jilted in the scandal of the Season. Longing for an escape from all the whispers and humiliation, Alice eagerly accepts an invitation to her friend's house party. In the country, she hopes to find some peace from the embarrassment left in London… Unfortunately, she finds her former betrothed and his new bride in attendance.

Never love a lady…

Lord Rhys Brookfield has no interest in marriage. Ever. He's worked quite hard at building both his fortune and his reputation as a rogue—and intends to enjoy all that they can offer him. That is if his match-making mother will stop pairing him with prospective brides. When Rhys and Alice meet, sparks flare. But with every new encounter, their first impressions of one another are challenged and an unlikely friendship is forged.

Desperate, Rhys proposes a pretend courtship, one meant to spite Alice's former betrothed and prevent any matchmaking attempts toward Rhys. What neither expects is that a pretense can become so much more. Or that a burning passion can heal… and hurt.

BEGUILED BY A BARON
Book 14 in the "Heart of a Duke" Series by Christi Caldwell

A Lady with a Secret… Partially deaf, with a birthmark marring her face, Bridget Hamilton is content with her life, even if she's been cast out of her family. But her peaceful existence—expanding her mind with her study of rare books—is threatened with an ultimatum from her evil brother—steal a valuable book or give up her son. Bridget has no choice; her son is her world.

A Lord with a Purpose… Vail Basingstoke, Baron Chilton is known throughout London as the Bastard Baron. After battling at Waterloo, he establishes himself as the foremost dealer in rare books and builds a fortune, determined to never be like the self-serving duke who sired him. He devotes his life to growing his fortune to care for his illegitimate siblings, also fathered by the duke. The chance to sell a highly coveted book for a financial windfall is his only thought.

Two Paths Collide… When Bridget masquerades as the baron's newest housekeeper, he's hopelessly intrigued by her quick wit and her skill with antique tomes. Wary from having his heart broken in the past, it should be easy enough to keep Bridget at arm's length, yet desire for her dogs his steps. As they spend time in each other's company, understanding for life grows as does love, but when Bridget's integrity is called into question, Vail's world is shattered—as is his heart again. Now Bridget and Vail will have to overcome the horrendous secrets and lies between them to grasp a love—and life—together.

TO ENCHANT A WICKED DUKE
Book 13 in the "Heart of a Duke" Series by Christi Caldwell

A Devil in Disguise

Years ago, when Nick Tallings, the recent Duke of Huntly, watched his family destroyed at the hands of a merciless nobleman, he vowed revenge. But his efforts had been futile, as his enemy, Lord Rutland is without weakness.

Until now…

With his rival finally happily married, Nick is able to set his ruthless scheme into motion. His plot hinges upon Lord Rutland's innocent, empty-headed sister-in-law, Justina Barrett. Nick will ruin her, marry her, and then leave her brokenhearted.

A Lady Dreaming of Love

From the moment Justina Barrett makes her Come Out, she is labeled a Diamond. Even with her ruthless father determined to sell her off to the highest bidder, Justina never gives up on her hope for a good, honorable gentleman who values her wit more than her looks.

A Not-So-Chance Meeting

Nick's ploy to ensnare Justina falls neatly into place in the streets of London. With each carefully orchestrated encounter, he slips further and further inside the lady's heart, never anticipating that Justina, with her quick wit and strength, will break down his own defenses. As Nick's plans begins to unravel, he's left to determine which is more important—Justina's love or his vow for vengeance. But can Justina ever forgive the duke who deceived her?

ONE WINTER WITH A BARON
Book 12 in the "Heart of a Duke" Series by Christi Caldwell

A clever spinster:

Content with her spinster lifestyle, Miss Sybil Cunning wants to prove that a future as an unmarried woman is the only life for her. As a bluestocking who values hard, empirical data, Sybil needs help with her research. Nolan Pratt, Baron Webb, one of society's most scandalous rakes, is the perfect gentleman to help her. After all, he inspires fear in proper mothers and desire within their daughters.

A notorious rake:

Society may be aware of Nolan Pratt, Baron's Webb's wicked ways, but what he has carefully hidden is his miserable handling of his family's finances. When Sybil presents him the opportunity to earn much-needed funds, he can't refuse.

A winter to remember:

However, what begins as a business arrangement becomes something more and with every meeting, Sybil slips inside his heart. Can this clever woman look beneath the veneer of a coldhearted rake to see the man Nolan truly is?

To Redeem a Rake
Book 11 in the "Heart of a Duke" Series by Christi Caldwell

He's spent years scandalizing society.
Now, this rake must change his ways.

Society's most infamous scoundrel, Daniel Winterbourne, the Earl of Montfort, has been promised a small fortune if he can relinquish his wayward, carousing lifestyle. And behaving means he must also help find a respectable companion for his youngest sister—someone who will guide her and whom she can emulate. However, Daniel knows no such woman. But when he encounters a childhood friend, Daniel believes she may just be the answer to all of his problems.

Having been secretly humiliated by an unscrupulous blackguard years earlier, Miss Daphne Smith dreams of finding work at Ladies of Hope, an institution that provides an education for disabled women. With her sordid past and a disfigured leg, few opportunities arise for a woman such as she. Knowing Daniel's history, she wishes to avoid him, but working for his sister is exactly the stepping stone she needs.

Their attraction intensifies as Daniel and Daphne grow closer, preparing his sister for the London Season. But Daniel must resist his desire for a woman tarnished by scandal while Daphne is reminded of the boy she once knew. Can society's most notorious rake redeem his reputation and become the man Daphne deserves?

To Woo a Widow
Book 10 in the "Heart of a Duke" Series by Christi Caldwell

They see a brokenhearted widow.
She's far from shattered.

Lady Philippa Winston is never marrying again. After her late husband's cruelty that she kept so well hidden, she has no desire to search for love.

Years ago, Miles Brookfield, the Marquess of Guilford, made a frivolous vow he never thought would come to fruition—he promised to marry his mother's goddaughter if he was unwed by the age of thirty. Now, to his dismay, he's faced with honoring that pledge. But when he encounters the beautiful and intriguing Lady Philippa, Miles knows his true path in life. It's up to him to break down every belief Philippa carries about gentlemen, proving that not only is love real, but that he is the man deserving of her sheltered heart.

Will Philippa let down her guard and allow Miles to woo a widow in desperate need of his love?

The Lure of a Rake
Book 9 in the "Heart of a Duke" Series by Christi Caldwell

A Lady Dreaming of Love
Lady Genevieve Farendale has a scandalous past. Jilted at the

altar years earlier and exiled by her family, she's now returned to London to prove she can be a proper lady. Even though she's not given up on the hope of marrying for love, she's wary of trusting again. Then she meets Cedric Falcot, the Marquess of St. Albans whose seductive ways set her heart aflutter. But with her sordid history, Genevieve knows a rake can also easily destroy her.

An Unlikely Pairing

What begins as a chance encounter between Cedric and Genevieve becomes something more. As they continue to meet, passions stir. But with Genevieve's hope for true love, she fears Cedric will be unable to give up his wayward lifestyle. After all, Cedric has spent years protecting his heart, and keeping everyone out. Slowly, she chips away at all the walls he's built, but when he falters, Genevieve can't offer him redemption. Now, it's up to Cedric to prove to Genevieve that the love of a man is far more powerful than the lure of a rake.

To Trust a Rogue
Book 8 in the "Heart of a Duke" Series by Christi Caldwell

A rogue

Marcus, the Viscount Wessex has carefully crafted the image of rogue and charmer for Polite Society. Under that façade, however, dwells a man whose dreams were shattered almost eight years earlier by a young lady who captured his heart, pledged her love, and then left him, with nothing more than a curt note.

A widow

Eight years earlier, faced with no other choice, Mrs. Eleanor Collins, fled London and the only man she ever loved, Marcus, Viscount Wessex. She has now returned to serve as a companion for her elderly aunt with a daughter in tow. Even though they're next door neighbors, there is little reason for her to move in the same circles as Marcus, just in case, she vows to avoid him, for he reminds her of all she lost when she left.

Reunited

As their paths continue to cross, Marcus finds his desire for Eleanor just as strong, but he learned long ago she's not to be trusted. He will offer her a place in his bed, but not anything more. Only, Eleanor has no interest in this new, roguish man. The more time they spend together, the protective wall they've constructed to keep the other out, begin to break. With all the betrayals and secrets between them, Marcus has to open his heart again. And Eleanor must decide if it's ever safe to trust a rogue.

To Wed His Christmas Lady
Book 7 in the "Heart of a Duke" Series by Christi Caldwell

She's longing to be loved:

Lady Cara Falcot has only served one purpose to her loathsome father—to increase his power through a marriage to the future Duke of Billingsley. As such, she's built protective walls about her heart, and presents an icy facade to the world around her. Journeying home from her finishing school for the Christmas holidays, Cara's carriage is stranded during a winter storm. She's forced to tarry at a ramshackle inn, where she immediately antagonizes another patron—William.

He's avoiding his duty in favor of one last adventure:

William Hargrove, the Marquess of Grafton has wanted only one thing in life—to avoid the future match his parents would have him make to a cold, duke's daughter. He's returning home from a blissful eight years of traveling the world to see to his responsibilities. But when a winter storm interrupts his trip and lands him at a falling-down inn, he's forced to share company with a commanding Lady Cara who initially reminds him exactly of the woman he so desperately wants to avoid.

A Christmas snowstorm ushers in the spirit of the season:

At the holiday time, these two people who despise each other due to first perceptions are offered renewed beginnings and fresh starts. As this gruff stranger breaks down the walls she's built about herself, Cara has to determine whether she can truly open her heart to trusting that any man is capable of good and that she herself is capable of love. And William has to set aside all previous thoughts he's carried of the polished ladies like Cara, to be the man to show her that love.

THE HEART OF A SCOUNDREL
Book 6 in the "Heart of a Duke" Series by Christi Caldwell

Ruthless, wicked, and dark, the Marquess of Rutland rouses terror in the breast of ladies and nobleman alike. All Edmund wants in life is power. After he was publically humiliated by his one love Lady Margaret, he vowed vengeance, using Margaret's niece, as his pawn. Except, he's thwarted by another, more enticing target—Miss Phoebe Barrett.

Miss Phoebe Barrett knows precisely the shame she's been born to. Because her father is a shocking letch she's learned to form her own opinions on a person's worth. After a chance meeting with the Marquess of Rutland, she is captivated by the mysterious man. He, too, is a victim of society's scorn, but the more encounters she has with Edmund, the more she knows there is powerful depth and emotion to the jaded marquess.

The lady wreaks havoc on Edmund's plans for revenge and he finds he wants Phoebe, at all costs. As she's drawn into the darkness of his world, Phoebe risks being destroyed by Edmund's ruthlessness. And Phoebe who desires love at all costs, has to determine if she can ever truly trust the heart of a scoundrel.

TO LOVE A LORD
Book 5 in the "Heart of a Duke" Series by Christi Caldwell

All she wants is security:
The last place finishing school instructor Mrs. Jane Munroe belongs, is in polite Society. Vowing to never wed, she's been scuttled around from post to post. Now she finds herself in the Marquess of Waverly's household. She's never met a nobleman she

liked, and when she meets the pompous, arrogant marquess, she remembers why. But soon, she discovers Gabriel is unlike any gentleman she's ever known.

All he wants is a companion for his sister:

What Gabriel finds himself with instead, is a fiery spirited, bespectacled woman who entices him at every corner and challenges his age-old vow to never trust his heart to a woman. But… there is something suspicious about his sister's companion. And he is determined to find out just what it is.

All they need is each other:

As Gabriel and Jane confront the truth of their feelings, the lies and secrets between them begin to unravel. And Jane is left to decide whether or not it is ever truly safe to love a lord.

LOVED BY A DUKE
Book 4 in the "Heart of a Duke" Series by Christi Caldwell

For ten years, Lady Daisy Meadows has been in love with Auric, the Duke of Crawford. Ever since his gallant rescue years earlier, Daisy knew she was destined to be his Duchess. Unfortunately, Auric sees her as his best friend's sister and nothing more. But perhaps, if she can manage to find the fabled heart of a duke pendant, she will win over the heart of her duke.

Auric, the Duke of Crawford enjoys Daisy's company. The last thing he is interested in however, is pursuing a romance with a woman he's known since she was in leading strings. This season, Daisy is turning up in the oddest places and he cannot help but notice that she is no longer a girl. But Auric wouldn't do something as foolhardy as to fall in love with Daisy. He couldn't. Not with the guilt he carries over his past sins… Not when he has no right to her heart…But perhaps, just perhaps, she can forgive the past and trust that he'd forever cherish her heart—but will she let him?

THE LOVE OF A ROGUE
Book 3 in the "Heart of a Duke" Series by Christi Caldwell

Lady Imogen Moore hasn't had an easy time of it since she made her Come Out. With her betrothed, a powerful duke breaking it off to wed her sister, she's become the *tons* favorite piece of gossip. Never again wanting to experience the pain of a broken heart, she's resolved to make a match with a polite, respectable gentleman. The last thing she wants is another reckless rogue.

Lord Alex Edgerton has a problem. His brother, tired of Alex's carousing has charged him with chaperoning their remaining, unwed sister about *ton* events. Shopping? No, thank you. Attending the theatre? He'd rather be at Forbidden Pleasures with a scantily clad beauty upon his lap. The task of *chaperone* becomes even more of a bother when his sister drags along her dearest friend, Lady Imogen to social functions. The last thing he wants in his life is a young, innocent English miss.

Except, as Alex and Imogen are thrown together, passions flare and Alex comes to find he not only wants Imogen in his bed, but also in his heart. Yet now he must convince Imogen to risk all, on the heart of a rogue.

MORE THAN A DUKE
Book 2 in the "Heart of a Duke" Series by Christi Caldwell

Polite Society doesn't take Lady Anne Adamson seriously. However, Anne isn't just another pretty young miss. When she discovers her father betrayed her mother's love and her family descended into poverty, Anne comes up with a plan to marry a respectable, powerful, and honorable gentleman—a man nothing like her philandering father.

Armed with the heart of a duke pendant, fabled to land the wearer a duke's heart, she decides to enlist the aid of the notorious

Harry, 6th Earl of Stanhope. A scoundrel with a scandalous past, he is the last gentleman she'd ever wed…however, his reputation marks him the perfect man to school her in the art of seduction so she might ensnare the illustrious Duke of Crawford.

Harry, the Earl of Stanhope is a jaded, cynical rogue who lives for his own pleasures. Having been thrown over by the only woman he ever loved so she could wed a duke, he's not at all surprised when Lady Anne approaches him with her scheme to capture another duke's affection. He's come to appreciate that all women are in fact greedy, title-grasping, self-indulgent creatures. And with Anne's history of grating on his every last nerve, she is the last woman he'd ever agree to school in the art of seduction. Only his friendship with the lady's sister compels him to help.

What begins as a pretend courtship, born of lessons on seduction, becomes something more leaving Anne to decide if she can give her heart to a reckless rogue, and Harry must decide if he's willing to again trust in a lady's love.

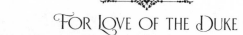

FOR LOVE OF THE DUKE
First Full-Length Book in the "Heart of a Duke" Series
by Christi Caldwell

After the tragic death of his wife, Jasper, the 8th Duke of Bainbridge buried himself away in the dark cold walls of his home, Castle Blackwood. When he's coaxed out of his self-imposed exile to attend the amusements of the Frost Fair, his life is irrevocably changed by his fateful meeting with Lady Katherine Adamson.

With her tight brown ringlets and silly white-ruffled gowns, Lady Katherine Adamson has found her dance card empty for two Seasons. After her father's passing, Katherine learned the unreliability of men, and is determined to depend on no one, except herself. Until she meets Jasper…

In a desperate bid to avoid a match arranged by her family, Katherine makes the Duke of Bainbridge a shocking proposition—one that he accepts.

Only, as Katherine begins to love Jasper, she finds the arrangement agreed upon is not enough. And Jasper is left to decide if protecting his heart is more important than fighting for Katherine's love.

IN NEED OF A DUKE
A Prequel Novella to "The Heart of a Duke" Series
by Christi Caldwell

In Need of a Duke: (Author's Note: This is a prequel novella to "The Heart of a Duke" series by Christi Caldwell. It was originally available in "The Heart of a Duke" Collection and is now being published as an individual novella.

~★~

It features a new prologue and epilogue.

Years earlier, a gypsy woman passed to Lady Aldora Adamson and her friends a heart pendant that promised them each the heart of a duke.

Now, a young lady, with her family facing ruin and scandal, Lady Aldora doesn't have time for mythical stories about cheap baubles. She needs to save her sisters and brother by marrying a titled gentleman with wealth and power to his name. She sets her bespectacled sights upon the Marquess of St. James.

Turned out by his father after a tragic scandal, Lord Michael Knightly has grown into a powerful, but self-made man. With the whispers and stares that still follow him, he would rather be anywhere but London...

Until he meets Lady Aldora, a young woman who mistakes him for his brother, the Marquess of St. James. The connection between Aldora and Michael is immediate and as they come to know one another, Aldora's feelings for Michael war with her sisterly responsibilities. With her family's dire situation, a man of Michael's scandalous past will never do.

Ultimately, Aldora must choose between her responsibilities as a sister and her love for Michael.

Once a Wallflower, At Last His Love
Book 6 in the Scandalous Seasons Series

Responsible, practical Miss Hermione Rogers, has been crafting stories as the notorious Mr. Michael Michaelmas and selling them for a meager wage to support her siblings. The only real way to ensure her family's ruinous debts are paid, however, is to marry. Tall, thin, and plain, she has no expectation of success. In London for her first Season she seizes the chance to write the tale of a brooding duke. In her research, she finds Sebastian Fitzhugh, the 5th Duke of Mallen, who unfortunately is perfectly affable, charming, and so nicely… configured… he takes her breath away. He lacks all the character traits she needs for her story, but alas, any duke will have to do.

Sebastian Fitzhugh, the 5th Duke of Mallen has been deceived so many times during the high-stakes game of courtship, he's lost faith in Society women. Yet, after a chance encounter with Hermione, he finds himself intrigued. Not a woman he'd normally consider beautiful, the young lady's practical bent, her forthright nature and her tendency to turn up in the oddest places has his interests… roused. He'd like to trust her, he'd like to do a whole lot more with her too, but should he?

A Marquess For Christmas
Book 5 in the Scandalous Seasons Series

Lady Patrina Tidemore gave up on the ridiculous notion of true love after having her heart shattered and her trust destroyed by a black-hearted cad. Used as a pawn in a game of revenge against her brother, Patrina returns to London from a failed elopement with a tattered reputation and little hope for a respectable match. The only peace she finds is in her solitude on the cold winter days at Hyde Park. And even that is yanked from her by two little hellions who just happen to have a devastatingly handsome, but coldly aloof father, the Marquess of Beaufort. Something about the lord stirs the dreams she'd once carried for an honorable gentleman's love.

Weston Aldridge, the 4th Marquess of Beaufort was deceived and betrayed by his late wife. In her faithlessness, he's come to view women as self-serving, indulgent creatures. Except, after a series of chance encounters with Patrina, he comes to appreciate how uniquely different she is than all women he's ever known.

At the Christmastide season, a time of hope and new beginnings, Patrina and Weston, unexpectedly learn true love in one another. However, as Patrina's scandalous past threatens their future and the happiness of his children, they are both left to determine if love is enough.

ALWAYS A ROGUE, FOREVER HER LOVE
Book 4 in the Scandalous Seasons Series

Miss Juliet Marshville is spitting mad. With one guardian missing, and the other singularly uninterested in her fate, she is at the mercy of her wastrel brother who loses her beloved childhood home to a man known as Sin. Determined to reclaim control of Rosecliff Cottage and her own fate, Juliet arranges a meeting with the notorious rogue and demands the return of her property.

Jonathan Tidemore, 5th Earl of Sinclair, known to the *ton* as Sin, is exceptionally lucky in life and at the gaming tables. He has just one problem. Well…four, really. His incorrigible sisters have driven off yet another governess. This time, however, his mother demands he find an appropriate replacement.

When Miss Juliet Marshville boldly demands the return of her precious cottage, he takes advantage of his sudden good fortune and puts an offer to her; turn his sisters into proper English ladies, and he'll return Rosecliff Cottage to Juliet's possession.

Jonathan comes to appreciate Juliet's spirit, courage, and clever wit, and decides to claim the fiery beauty as his mistress. Juliet, however, will be mistress for no man. Nor could she ever love a man who callously stole her home in a game of cards. As Jonathan begins to see Juliet as more than a spirited beauty to warm his bed, he realizes she could be a lady he could love the rest of his life, if only he can convince the proud Juliet that he's worthy of her hand and heart.

ALWAYS PROPER, SUDDENLY SCANDALOUS
Book 3 in the Scandalous Seasons Series

Geoffrey Winters, Viscount Redbrooke was not always the hard, unrelenting lord driven by propriety. After a tragic mistake, he resolved to honor his responsibility to the Redbrooke line and live a life, free of scandal. Knowing his duty is to wed a proper, respectable English miss, he selects Lady Beatrice Dennington, daughter of the Duke of Somerset, the perfect woman for him. Until he meets Miss Abigail Stone…

To distance herself from a personal scandal, Abigail Stone flees America to visit her uncle, the Duke of Somerset. Determined to never trust a man again, she is helplessly intrigued by the hard, too-proper Geoffrey. With his strict appreciation for decorum and order, he is nothing like the man' she's always dreamed of.

Abigail is everything Geoffrey does not need. She upends his carefully ordered world at every encounter. As they begin to care for one another, Abigail carefully guards the secret that resulted in her journey to England.

Only, if Geoffrey learns the truth about Abigail, he must decide which he holds most dear: his place in Society or Abigail's place in his heart.

NEVER COURTED, SUDDENLY WED
Book 2 in the Scandalous Seasons Series

Christopher Ansley, Earl of Waxham, has constructed a perfect image for the *ton*–the ladies love him and his company is desired by all. Only two people know the truth about Waxham's secret. Unfortunately, one of them is Miss Sophie Winters.

Sophie Winters has known Christopher since she was in leading strings. As children, they delighted in tormenting each other. Now at two and twenty, she still has a tendency to find herself in scrapes, and her marital prospects are slim.

When his father threatens to expose his shame to the *ton*, unless he weds Sophie for her dowry, Christopher concocts a plan to remain a bachelor. What he didn't plan on was falling in love with the lively, impetuous Sophie. As secrets are exposed, will Christopher's love be enough when she discovers his role in his father's scheme?

FOREVER BETROTHED, NEVER THE BRIDE
Book 1 in the Scandalous Seasons Series

Hopeless romantic Lady Emmaline Fitzhugh is tired of sitting with the wallflowers, waiting for her betrothed to come to his senses and marry her. When Emmaline reads one too many reports of his scandalous liaisons in the gossip rags, she takes matters into her own hands.

War-torn veteran Lord Drake devotes himself to forgetting his days on the Peninsula through an endless round of meaningless associations. He no longer wants to feel anything, but Lady Emmaline is making it hard to maintain a state of numbness. With her zest for life, she awakens his passion and desire for love.

The one woman Drake has spent the better part of his life avoiding is now the only woman he needs, but he is no longer a man worthy of his Emmaline. It is up to her to show him the healing power of love.

A SEASON OF HOPE
A Danby Novella

Five years ago when her love, Marcus Wheatley, failed to return from fighting Napoleon's forces, Lady Olivia Foster buried her heart. Unable to betray Marcus's memory, Olivia has gone out of her way to run off prospective suitors. At three and twenty she considers herself firmly on the shelf. Her father, however, disagrees and accepts an offer for Olivia's hand in marriage. Yet it's Christmas, when anything can happen…

Olivia receives a well-timed summons from her grandfather, the Duke of Danby, and eagerly embraces the reprieve from her betrothal.

Only, when Olivia arrives at Danby Castle she realizes the Christmas season represents hope, second chances, and even miracles.

"WINNING A LADY'S HEART"
A Danby Novella

Author's Note: This is a novella that was originally available in A Summons From The Castle (The Regency Christmas Summons Collection). It is being published as an individual novella.

~★~

For Lady Alexandra, being the source of a cold, calculated wager is bad enough…but when it is waged by Nathaniel Michael Winters, 5th Earl of Pembroke, the man she's in love with, it results in a broken heart, the scandal of the season, and a summons from her grandfather – the Duke of Danby.

To escape Society's gossip, she hurries to her meeting with the duke, determined to put memories of the earl far behind. Except the duke has other plans for Alexandra…plans which include the 5th Earl of Pembroke!

TEMPTED BY A LADY'S SMILE
Book 4 in the "Lords of Honor" Series

Richard Jonas has loved but one woman—a woman who belongs to his brother. Refusing to suffer any longer, he evades his family in order to barricade his heart from unrequited love. While attending a friend's summer party, Richard's approach to love is changed after sharing a passionate and life-altering kiss with a vibrant and mysterious woman. Believing he was incapable of loving again, Richard finds himself tempted by a young lady determined to marry his best friend.

Gemma Reed has not been treated kindly by the *ton*. Often disregarded for her appearance and interests unlike those of a proper lady, Gemma heads to house party to win the heart of Lord Westfield, the man she's loved for years. But her plan is set off course by the tempting and intriguing, Richard Jonas.

A chance meeting creates a new path for Richard and Gemma to forage—but can two people, scorned and shunned by those they've loved from afar, let down their guards to find true happiness?

"RESCUED BY A LADY'S LOVE"
Book 3 in the "Lords of Honor" Series

Destitute and determined to finally be free of any man's shackles, Lily Benedict sets out to salvage her honor. With no choice but to commit a crime that will save her from her past, she enters the home of the recluse, Derek Winters, the new Duke of Blackthorne. But entering the "Beast of Blackthorne's" lair proves more threatening than she ever imagined.

With half a face and a mangled leg, Derek—once rugged and charming—only exists within the confines of his home. Shunned by society, Derek is leery of the hauntingly beautiful Lily Benedict. As time passes, she slips past his defenses, reminding him how to live again. But when Lily's sordid past comes back, threatening her life, it's up to Derek to find the strength to become the hero he once was. Can they overcome the darkness of their sins to find a life of love and redemption?

CAPTIVATED BY A LADY'S CHARM
Book 2 in the "Lords of Honor" Series

In need of a wife...

Christian Villiers, the Marquess of St. Cyr, despises the role he's been cast into as fortune hunter but requires the funds to keep his marquisate solvent. Yet, the sins of his past cloud his future, preventing him from seeing beyond his fateful actions at the Battle of Toulouse. For he knows inevitably it will catch up with him, and everyone will remember his actions on the battlefield that cost so many so much—particularly his best friend.

In want of a husband...

Lady Prudence Tidemore's life is plagued by familial scandals, which makes her own marital prospects rather grim. Surely there is one gentleman of the ton who can look past her family and see just her and all she has to offer?

When Prudence runs into Christian on a London street, the charming, roguish gentleman immediately captures her attention. But then a chance meeting becomes a waltz, and now...

A Perfect Match...

All she must do is convince Christian to forget the cold requirements he has for his future marchioness. But the demons in his past prevent him from turning himself over to love. One thing is certain—Prudence wants the marquess and is determined to have him in her life, now and forever. It's just a matter of convincing Christian he wants the same.

SEDUCED BY A LADY'S HEART
Book 1 in the "Lords of Honor" Series

You met Lieutenant Lucien Jones in "Forever Betrothed, Never the Bride" when he was a broken soldier returned from fighting Boney's forces. This is his story of triumph and happily-ever-after!

Lieutenant Lucien Jones, son of a viscount, returned from war, to find his wife and child dead. Blaming his father for the commission that sent him off to fight Boney's forces, he was content to languish at London Hospital... until offered employment on the Marquess of Drake's staff. Through his position, Lucien found purpose in life and is content to keep his past buried.

Lady Eloise Yardley has loved Lucien since they were children. Having long ago given up on the dream of him, she married another. Years later, she is a young, lonely widow who does not fit in with the ton. When Lucien's family enlists her aid to reunite father and son, she leaps at the opportunity to not only aid her former friend, but to also escape London.

Lucien doesn't know what scheme Eloise has concocted, but knowing her as he does, when she pays a visit to his employer, he knows she's up to something. The last thing he wants is the temptation that this new, older, mature Eloise presents; a tantalizing reminder of happier times and peace.

Yet Eloise is determined to win Lucien's love once and for all... if only Lucien can set aside the pain of his past and risk all on a lady's heart.

◠Only For Their Love
Book 3 in the "The Theodosia Sword" Series

Miss Carol Cresswall bore witness to her parents' loveless union and is determined to avoid that same miserable fate. Her mother has altogether different plans—plans that include a match between Carol and Lord Gregory Renshaw. Despite his wealth and power, Carol has no interest in marrying a pompous man who goes out of his way to ignore her. Now, with their families coming together for the Christmastide season it's her mother's last-ditch effort to get them together. And Carol plans to avoid Gregory at all costs.

Lord Gregory Renshaw has no intentions of falling prey to his mother's schemes to marry him off to a proper debutante she's picked out. Over the years, he has carefully sidestepped all endeavors to be matched with any of the grasping ladies.

But a sudden Christmastide Scandal has the potential show Carol and Gregory that they've spent years running from the one thing they've always needed.

ONLY FOR HER HONOR
Book 2 in the "The Theodosia Sword" Series

A wounded soldier:

When Captain Lucas Rayne returned from fighting Boney's forces, he was a shell of a man. A recluse who doesn't leave his family's estate, he's content to shut himself away. Until he meets Eve…

A woman alone in the world:

Eve Ormond spent most of her life following the drum alongside her late father. When his shameful actions bring death and pain to English soldiers, Eve is forced back to England, an outcast. With no family or marital prospects she needs employment and finds it in Captain Lucas Rayne's home. A man whose life was ruined by her father, Eve has no place inside his household. With few options available, however, Eve takes the post. What she never anticipates is how with their every meeting, this honorable, hurting soldier slips inside her heart.

The Secrets Between Them:

The more time Lucas spends with Eve, he remembers what it is to be alive and he lets the walls protecting his heart down. When the secrets between them come to light will their love be enough? Or are they two destined for heartbreak?

ONLY FOR HIS LADY
Book 1 in the "The Theodosia Sword" Series

A curse. A sword. And the thief who stole her heart.

The Rayne family is trapped in a rut of bad luck. And now, it's up to Lady Theodosia Rayne to steal back the Theodosia sword, a gladius that was pilfered by the rival, loathed Renshaw family. Hopefully, recovering the stolen sword will break the cycle and reverse her family's fate.

Damian Renshaw, the Duke of Devlin, is feared by all—all, that is, except Lady Theodosia, the brazen spitfire who enters his home and wrestles an ancient relic from his wall. Intrigued by the vivacious woman, Devlin has no intentions of relinquishing the sword to her.

As Theodosia and Damian battle for ownership, passion ignites. Now, they are torn between their age-old feud and the fire that burns between them. Can two forbidden lovers find a way to make amends before their families' war tears them apart?

My Lady of Deception
Book 1 in the "Brethren of the Lords" Series

This dark, sweeping Regency novel was previously only offered as part of the limited edition box sets: "From the Ballroom and Beyond", "Romancing the Rogue", and "Dark Deceptions". Now, available for the first time on its own, exclusively through Amazon is "My Lady of Deception".

~★~

Everybody has a secret. Some are more dangerous than others.

For Georgina Wilcox, only child of the notorious traitor known as "The Fox", there are too many secrets to count. However, after her interference results in great tragedy, she resolves to never help another... until she meets Adam Markham.

Lord Adam Markham is captured by The Fox. Imprisoned, Adam loses everything he holds dear. As his days in captivity grow, he finds himself fascinated by the young maid, Georgina, who cares for him.

When the carefully crafted lies she's built between them begin to crumble, Georgina realizes she will do anything to prove her love and loyalty to Adam—even it means at the expense of her own life.

NON-FICTION WORKS BY
CHRISTI CALDWELL

**Uninterrupted Joy: Memoir: My Journey through
Infertility, Pregnancy, and Special Needs**

The following journey was never intended for publication.
It was written from a mother, to her unborn child. The words
detailed her struggle through infertility and the joy of finally being
pregnant. A stunning revelation at her son's birth opened a world
of both fear and discovery. This is the story of one mother's love
and hope and…her quest for uninterrupted joy.

BIOGRAPHY

Christi Caldwell is the bestselling author of historical romance novels set in the Regency era. Christi blames Judith McNaught's "Whitney, My Love," for luring her into the world of historical romance. While sitting in her graduate school apartment at the University of Connecticut, Christi decided to set aside her notes and try her hand at writing romance. She believes the most perfect heroes and heroines have imperfections and rather enjoys tormenting them before crafing a well-deserved happily ever after!

When Christi isn't writing the stories of flawed heroes and heroines, she can be found in her Southern Connecticut home chasing around her eight-year-old son, and caring for twin princesses-in-training!

Visit *www.christicaldwellauthor.com* to learn more about what Christi is working on, or join her on Facebook at Christi Caldwell Author, and Twitter @ChristiCaldwell

Made in the USA
San Bernardino, CA
10 January 2019